Cupid's Curse
By
Kathi Daley

This book is dedicated to my valentine, the "real" Zak, my best friend and superhusband Ken, who has been taking care of all my needs, before I even know I have a need, for the past thirty-five years.

I also want to give a special shout-out to Squeaky, a little guy with a big heart who touched a lot of lives.

Special thanks to all my Facebook friends who share their opinions and encouragement, with a special thanks to Jade K. and Tamara M., an aunt-and-niece team who tried some of the recipes in the backs of the books and posted their results.

And, as always, thank you to my sister Christy for her encouragement and valuable feedback, Ricky for the webpage, and Randy Ladenheim-Gil for the editing.

Books by Kathi Daley

Buy them on Amazon today.

Paradise Lake Series:
Pumpkins in Paradise
Snowmen in Paradise
Bikinis in Paradise
Christmas in Paradise
Puppies in Paradise – *February 2015*

Zoe Donovan Mysteries:
Halloween Hijinks
The Trouble With Turkeys
Christmas Crazy
Cupid's Curse
Big Bunny Bump-off
Beach Blanket Barbie
Maui Madness
Derby Divas
Haunted Hamlet
Turkeys, Tuxes, and Tabbies
Christmas Cozy – *November 2014*
Alaskan Alliance – *December 2014*

Road to Christmas Romance:
Road to Christmas Past

Chapter 1

Sunday, February 2

"Zoe, are you okay?" My father, Hank Donovan, asked as I stared into eyes as blue as my own with my mouth hanging open in shock. "I know this might seem sort of sudden."

"Sudden?" I gasped. "Are you kidding me? You've known this woman two months and we're seriously sitting here discussing the possibility of you moving in with her?"

"It's been three months," Dad corrected. "And I didn't say I was going to do it. I just wanted you to know that she approached me with the idea and I'm considering it."

I sat back, took a deep breath, and counted to ten. My dad is normally a conservative and logical person. I knew that his involvement with my mother a few months ago, and her subsequent desertion for the second time in his life, had greatly affected him, but until this moment I really had no idea how much the status quo had been irreparably altered. I leaned forward in the restaurant booth we shared and placed my hand over his across the table. For the first time, I noticed that his dark hair was thinning a bit, and the scattering of gray was becoming more predominant. Although my dad was still an attractive and energetic man, he *had* turned forty-seven on his birthday last month, and it occurred to me that he might be experiencing the syndrome men his age seemed destined to encounter: the midlife crisis.

"I understand you might want to pursue a romantic relationship, but I think it's much too soon for you to consider such a big step. Perhaps you should slow things down, take a step back, and have another look at the situation. I'm sorry, but I really don't think this is a good idea at all."

Dad squeezed my hand and looked me directly in the eye. "Zoe, you know I love you, but in case you've forgotten, *I* am the parent and *you* are the child. I'm not here to ask your permission, only to inform you of my situation. If and when I decide it's time to move in with Blythe—or anyone else, for that matter—I can assure you that I'll be making the decision on my own."

Ouch. That really hurt. Dad and I had always been close, but somehow I felt like I was having lunch with a stranger. How had we gotten to this point? My mom had been out of the picture since just after I was born, and my dad had raised me alone. We'd always been the two musketeers and I thought that had been enough for him. He'd never really dated, seeming content with his lot in life, until my mom unexpectedly returned the previous summer and tilted Dad off his axis. I don't know everything that occurred, but I do know that the encounter affected him in a profound way. He hadn't been the same content and carefree man since she'd left just before Halloween.

I wanted to plead with him to reconsider his relationship with the new woman in town, who I hated quite a lot, but just as I was about to launch into my briefly rehearsed tirade, the witch in question walked through the front door of the café and headed toward us. I pulled back my hand and leaned into the red vinyl cushion behind me, folding my arms across my chest like a petulant child.

"Blythe," I sneered, as my inner, eight-year-old brat reared her ugly head.

"Zoe, dear, do sit up straight. You're slouching. Not at all an attractive look for a young woman of your age."

I ignored the woman and slouched further into the booth to the point where I could barely see over the top of the table. Of course, given the fact that I am a mere five feet tall, I really didn't have to squash down all that much to accomplish this feat.

"I've made you an appointment with my hairdresser in the valley. He's absolutely the best. I just know you'll be a beautiful woman if we can manage a way to tame all those curls."

"I like my curls," I said.

"Yes, well, I'm sure they're perfectly lovely. For a child. You're twenty-four, my dear. It's time to start looking like an adult."

"The curls stay," I insisted. Blythe had been commenting on my hair since the day I met her. The more she pushed for a change, the more determined I became to keep things the same.

"I guess we'll see about that. Has your father told you our news?"

I clenched my fists and considered the penalty for assault as Charlie, my half Tibetan terrier/half mystery dog, who was sitting quietly at my feet, began to growl. Charlie is very sensitive to my moods, and I was certain he sensed my level of distress.

Blythe looked under the table. "Oh, Zoe, did you bring that filthy animal with you again? I'm sure you realize that a restaurant is no place for a dog."

I'm quite certain my face turned red and steam began to pour out of my ears at that point. It's one thing to criticize me, but as far as I'm concerned, *no one* messes with my dog.

"Charlie is a therapy dog," my dad contributed. "He's extremely well behaved, and Zoe bathes him quite regularly. I don't think anyone considers it a problem for him to be here."

"You really shouldn't coddle the child the way you do. She needs to learn manners and proper etiquette."

"Hello." I sat up. "I'm right here. Didn't anyone ever tell you it was impolite to talk about people as if they weren't there?"

"Yes, dear. I'm sure you're right. I do apologize. Now, about that haircut . . . I thought we could add some highlights as well. All that brown detracts from your lovely complexion, and I'm certain a touch of blond will bring out the blue in your eyes."

"Good afternoon, Ms. Ravenwood," our waitress, and my best friend, Ellie Davis interrupted, saving me from having to reply. If I know Ellie, and I do, I'm sure she'd witnessed our altercation and hurried over before muffins started to fly. For those of you who don't know me, I tend to be extremely protective of my relationships and as a result am prone to unreasonable acts of jealousy and spontaneous displays of childishness. I hate to admit it, but it really doesn't take a lot to set me off, and Blythe's total power over my dad, coupled with her attempt to manipulate me, was about to catapult me into a food-throwing frenzy.

"Would you like to order something?" Ellie asked.

"Why, yes, dear. Don't you look nice today? Is that a new haircut?"

"Yes; thank you for noticing." Ellie smiled. She had cut her straight, waist-length brown hair to an attractive shoulder length a few days before. I had to admit the style suited her, as it tended to emphasize her thin face, porcelain complexion, and huge brown eyes.

"Well, it's simply adorable. You look so mature and sophisticated. The right haircut can make all the difference." Blyth glanced at me, and I had to use every ounce of self-control to keep from sticking my tongue out at her.

"Can I get you something?" Ellie slid me a warning look. She knows my feelings for the woman who is campaigning to be my evil stepmother are irrational at best.

"Perhaps a cup of tea." Blythe graced Ellie with the most disgusting sugar-and-nice smile I'd ever seen. "What variety would you recommend?"

"We have a nice peppermint spice," Ellie offered.

"What a wonderful suggestion. That sounds perfect."

Okay, now I know Blythe is only being übernice to Ellie to get under my skin. I'm sure you can see it as well. And everyone thinks *I'm* the manipulative and irrational one.

"I really have to go." I slid out of the booth as Ellie walked away. "We'll talk later," I promised my dad. I turned to leave when a rather large man in a black silk shirt with brass buttons walked up behind me, completely blocking my way. Talk about being stuck in the seventies.

"Adriana?" He looked directly at the demon sitting next to my father.

"I'm afraid you're mistaken." Blythe turned an unusual shade of red.

"Yeah, right. You have a minute?"

"I'm afraid you have the wrong woman," my dad spoke up.

The man glanced at Blythe and then at my dad. He frowned and then shrugged. "Yeah, I guess I do. I'm sorry for the interruption."

He turned and walked back out of the front door.

"That was odd," I murmured. I couldn't help but notice that Blythe looked extremely uncomfortable about the encounter.

"Yes, well, these things happen." Blythe looked at my dad and smiled. "Perhaps we should be going. We don't want to be late for the movie."

"It doesn't start for two hours," my dad pointed out.

"I've decided to stop by my place to change." Blythe slid out of the booth without waiting for my dad's assent. She turned and walked toward the front door.

"I guess we're leaving." My dad followed her out of the booth. "We'll talk some more another time."

"Count on it."

After they left, Ellie came back to the table with Blythe's tea. "They left?"

"Apparently," I answered in a voice snarkier than was really called for.

"I had to be nice to her," Ellie defended. "It's my job."

I looked at my best friend in the whole world. The fact that Blythe and her relationship with my father had catapulted me out of my comfort zone really wasn't her fault. To be honest, she'd been nothing but supportive of my feelings since the wicked stepwitch moved to town. "I know," I admitted. "I'm just being Zoe."

"I overheard a bit of your conversation with your dad. He's really thinking of moving in with her?" Ellie asked as she began clearing the table.

"He says he's considering the idea," I admitted as Charlie and I followed her back to the kitchen. "Have you ever heard of such a ridiculous idea? He's only known her a few months. I'm afraid he may have fallen into the midlife sinkhole."

"Sinkhole?" Ellie laughed as she began sorting the dishes for washing.

"Do you have a better explanation?"

"Your dad has been single his whole life. He's devoted all his energy to you, but now you've grown up and have your own life. It's natural that he'd be looking for a companion at this point. Besides, I think it was really hard on him when your mom showed up out of the blue and then left just as abruptly. If you want my advice, I'd give him a break. He's always been there for you. Perhaps it's time to return the favor. If Blythe makes him happy, maybe you should try harder to get along with her."

Ellie was right. My dad *had* always been there for me, and Blythe *did* seem to make him happy. Truth be told, I probably would hate any woman my dad developed a serious relationship with, even if she weren't the world's most irritating woman. As I've mentioned before, I have been known to display irrational feelings of jealousy toward anyone who interferes in my closest relationships. Maybe it was time for me to grow up and stop acting like a spoiled child.

"Do you want to come over for dinner tonight?"

Ellie hesitated. "I'd love to have dinner with you, but I sort of made plans with Rob and some of the members of the group."

Rob was a single father who'd started a group for single parents. They often did things socially, as well as trading babysitting and offering support.

"You aren't a single parent," I reminded her.

"I know, but I find being with the group to be enjoyable, and they've totally accepted me as one of their own, in spite of the fact I'm short at least one child. It's probably because of all the free babysitting I provide, but I'm having fun with them, and you've been otherwise occupied of late."

I guess I hadn't stopped to consider the effect my relationship with my ex-enemy and current neighbor and boyfriend Zak Zimmerman might have on Ellie. Zak and I had been together every night since Christmas, until he left a few days ago for a business trip to the East Coast.

"We're going bowling. You're welcome to come, if you want," Ellie offered.

"Thanks, but I think I'll pass."

"Is Zak still out of town?"

"Yeah. He said he would be back for the grand opening of Zoe's Zoo on Thursday." Zoe's Zoo is the animal adoption and rehabilitation shelter that Zak bought for me after the county fired me as an animal control officer and closed the local facility. We've been waiting for operating permits for over two months. Unless something goes seriously wrong, it looks like we're *finally* set to open in a few short days.

"You sound . . ." Ellie searched for the right emotion, "concerned?"

"Zak didn't ask me to watch Lambda." Lambda is Zak's dog.

"Did he take him?"

"No. He said that a friend was staying at the mansion and he was going to leave Lambda behind to keep his friend company."

"Makes sense," Ellie concluded. "So why the doom and gloom?"

"He's been really secretive and has gone out of his way not to mention *who* it is that's staying with him. He even uses gender-neutral tags when speaking of this individual, so I figure it must be a female guest. The last time someone stayed at his house, it was his beautiful business partner, Belinda."

"Did you ask him who was staying with him?" Ellie quite reasonably asked.

"No. Not directly," I admitted. "I didn't want to seem needy."

"But you *are* needy."

"I know." I sighed. I've really been working on holstering Zoe the Jealous, but after years of nurturing her, it's been a hard transition. "I was sort of hoping he'd tell me who his guest was on his own. I gave him plenty of opportunity to do so, but he was purposely vague, and when I offered to stop by to check on things while he was away, he told me that his guest really wanted solitude and privacy in order to work through some personal issues."

Ellie smiled. "Look on the bright side. If Belinda is staying at his house, she isn't on the East Coast with him."

"Good point." Suddenly I felt a lot better "Maybe I'll see if Levi wants to hang out tonight. Zak's only been gone a few days, and I've been making myself nuts trying to figure out why he's been so secretive. I could use a distraction."

"I'm sure he'd love to hang out with you if you can tear him away from his plastic girlfriend."

"Meow. Apparently, I'm not the only one with relationship issues."

Levi Denton is the other member of the Zoe, Levi, and Ellie trio. The three of us have been best friends since kindergarten, when our teacher sat the class at round tables of three by last name. Levi has been dating a woman by the name of Barbie, who has a figure resembling her doll counterpart, for the past few months, and Ellie has made no secret about the fact that she doesn't approve of that relationship.

"Levi and I don't have relationship issues," Ellie insisted. "It's just that . . ." Ellie paused, a concerned look crossing her face. "Do you think they're really going to move in together?"

"I don't know. Levi *did* go with her to visit her family over Christmas, and she *has* been pushing the idea, so maybe."

"Maybe what?" Levi asked as he walked into the kitchen through the back door of Rosie's Café. Talk about perfect timing. Levi works at the local high school. An athletic jack-of-all-trades, he coaches football in the fall, basketball in the winter, and baseball in the spring. Levi is a handsome man: six foot two, with thick brown hair, sun-kissed skin from the hours he spends outdoors, and muscles that prove he walks his talk and pays a visit to the gym almost every day.

"*Maybe* you'd want to hang out with me tonight," I answered.

"I'd love to." Levi smiled. "You in as well?" He looked at Ellie.

Ellie hesitated. Although she's never admitted it to Levi, Ellie's feelings toward the man who had been like a brother to her for most of her life have changed over the past few months. Ellie has tried to keep her feelings to herself, but as her best friend, I knew that what were once friendly affections had grown into something more.

"Are you bringing Barbie?" Ellie asked.

"No. I think I could use a break from the fabulous B. A night with my two best friends sounds just about perfect. When was the last time we hung out, just the three of us?"

"I'm supposed to go bowling with Rob and the group," Ellie said.

"So reschedule. Come on, El, it won't be the same without you."

"Okay. I'll call Rob and tell him something came up."

"Fantastic." I smiled. What started off as a perfectly horrible day had just gotten a whole lot better. "Dinner at the boathouse?" I suggested.

"I'll bring the tequila," Levi offered.

"I'll bring the dinner," Ellie added.

"And I'll make a dessert."

After I left Rosie's, I decided I'd need a quick trip to the market if I was going to have ingredients for the dessert I'd promised. The day had started off sunny and bright, but during my time at the café, dark clouds had blown in over the summit and snow flurries were beginning to appear in the crisp air. I glanced at the large alpine lake that bordered the south side of Main Street. The clouds, which had appeared as if by magic, hung low over the water, completely concealing the landmass on the south shore. I loved days like this, when the lake looked more like an ocean and the isolation of my mountain home brought a feeling of oneness with the natural landscape.

The mom-and-pop shops that lined the north side of the main drag of Ashton Falls were decked out with white lights and red accents, in an effort to persuade casual shoppers to spend their hard-earned money on chocolate and roses. Valentine's Day was just around the corner, and while the annual holiday in Ashton Falls is pretty tame, local merchants decorate to entice visitors from the valley to buy tickets to the Chamber-sponsored Sweetheart Dance. In spite of the snow flurries, Charlie and I decided to make the short walk between Rosie's and the general store. There's something magical about walking along a snow-covered sidewalk illuminated with thousands of white twinkle lights hung in every tree and surrounding every window. The lights first appear in the fall and are left to bring warmth to the small town until the first sign of spring transitions the walkway with baskets of bright flowers.

As Charlie and I arrived at the store, we stopped to consider the boxed chocolates on display near the register. I have to admit I'm a sucker for anything with nuts or caramel. The candy was wrapped in large heart-shaped boxes, and while they *did* look tempting, I decided that making something would show more effort on my part, so I headed toward the aisle featuring baking supplies.

"Afternoon, Zoe, Charlie," grocery-store owner Ernie Young greeted me. "Looks like we're in for a spot of weather."

"Looks like."

"Heard talk that we might be looking at a full-on blizzard by the end of the week. Best stock up on canned goods just in case. Special on soup this week: ten cans for ten dollars."

Soup did sound good, and my cupboards were getting pretty bare, but the fact that Charlie and I had left our truck down the street caused me to reconsider.

"I really just need something for dessert tonight," I answered.

"I've got brownie mix on special."

"Brownies sound good."

After picking up a box of the double-nut variety of the chocolaty dessert, Charlie and I headed over to a display featuring pastries that were baked daily at Veronica's Bakery. I have to admit I have a sweet tooth, and it seemed quite reasonable to me that a chocolate treat would be the perfect thing to snack on while I baked the brownies for that evening.

"I picked up some of those éclair's last week," Hazel Hampton, our local librarian, commented as I contemplated a box of Veronica's delicious buttercreams. "They were the best I'd ever had."

"I'm making brownies for dessert tonight, but maybe one for the road." I picked up a package with a single pastry.

"So are you ready for your opening on Thursday?" Hazel asked about the long-awaited opening of Zoe's Zoo.

"More than ready."

"Remember to keep an eye out for a kitten for me."

"You'll be the first one we call if one is brought in."

"I like what you've done with the place," Hazel said, referring to the remodel we'd been working on since Zak had purchased the property from the county.

"You've seen it?"

"I stopped by the other day when Jeremy was there with Kevin Michaels and his new assistant. Those new cages you built in the back are going to be a godsend once our wildlife becomes active in the spring."

My assistant, Jeremy Fisher, had been putting in a lot of hours to ensure that Kevin got everything done in time for the opening. I had to agree with Hazel that the place looked awesome. Now if we could just get our final approval to occupy the space in time for the opening. It seemed like for every step forward we made in the process, something happened to cause us to take a step back. The community had been without a shelter since the county closed us down the previous November, and I knew I wasn't the only one anxious to get open for business.

"The new cages are going to allow us to house twice the number of large animals we used to," I confirmed. In addition to serving as a shelter for domestic animals such as dogs and cats, Zoe's Zoo planned to specialize in the care and rehabilitation of wild animals such as bears and coyotes as well. "I've already had a discussion with fish and game about taking over the care of those two cubs that were wounded in the Anderson fire. It seems the facility where they're currently being housed doesn't really have the infrastructure to provide long-term care."

"Excellent. It's always fun to have a bear on the property. Well, I guess I should get going. I'm taking a late lunch today, but I really need to get back. That new mystery novel you've been waiting for finally came in. I can hold it for you, if you want to stop by in the next day or two."

"Thanks. I'd appreciate that."

After we finished our shopping, Charlie and I headed home. We live in a converted boathouse that, along with the fifty acres of lakefront property that goes with it, is owned by my maternal grandfather, who originally used it to house his boat. I love my home. It's weathered and unconventional, with a large living area, a small loft bedroom, and a modern yet cozy kitchen. The entire wall facing the lake has been replaced with glass to give the space an open, airy feel. Off the front of the boathouse is a large deck, where I love to while away a summer afternoon or entertain guests. The little cove on which the boathouse was built is isolated from the main residential section of the lake, so when you're sitting on the deck, it feels like you have the entire lake to yourself.

I checked on my cats, Marlow and Spade, before building a fire in the river-rock fireplace and mixing together the brownies I'd bought and planned to serve with ice cream for dessert. While I considered my home to be primarily *my* space, I had made some concessions to the fact that Zak was spending the night more often, as evidenced by his shaving kit in the bathroom, his coffee mug on the rack, and extra clothes in the drawer I'd cleared for him in my dresser. Unlike my dad and Blythe and Levi and Barbie, who seemed ready to merge households after only a few dates, Zak and I have decided to take things slowly.

It had been snowing steadily the past few hours, so I put on knee-high boots and a heavy jacket and went out to shovel off the back deck, which had been added to the boathouse during the conversion and is separated from the lake by a good twenty feet of beach. When my grandfather originally built the boathouse, the water level of the lake was quite a bit higher, but nine years ago a group of farmers in the valley got together and challenged the legality of the Ashton Falls Dam. At the time the dam was built, water had been plentiful and everyone was happy, but after seven years of drought, the farm community at the foot of the mountain had been looking for a way to force the transfer of a greater amount of the runoff from the mountains directly to their crops. After winning an extremely messy lawsuit, the farmers had forced the opening of the dam, and the water level had decreased dramatically, effectively relocating the boathouse twenty feet from the natural waterline. Several years ago, I asked my mom if it would be possible for me to convert the abandoned structure and, surprisingly, my grandfather not only agreed but offered to pay for the renovation as well. Charlie and I have been living there ever since.

The high temperature for the day had been a blistering twenty-four degrees, causing my breath to condense as I worked to remove the four inches of fresh powder from the wooden surface. I paused after a few minutes to look out over the glassy water and take in the wonderful sound of absolute silence that can be found on a cold winter day. Once the deck was cleared, I headed back inside to check on the brownies, which had filled my little home with the most wonderful aroma. I turned some music on the stereo and tossed another log on the fire. If there was one thing that could be said for my cabin, it was that it provided cozy comfort when it was chilly outside. I was about to take off my boots when I heard a car pull up the front drive.

"Is there more?" I asked Ellie as she stomped the snow off her boots on the front deck.

"A couple more bags, but Levi pulled up behind me, so he's getting them."

"You have a lot of stuff. I figured you'd just bring soup or a casserole from Rosie's."

"I made shredded beef for our single-parent get-together yesterday and had a ton left, so I decided I'd heat it up, grate some cheese, heat some beans, and make burritos."

My mouth started to water. "Did you make guacamole?"

"Of course. I shredded some lettuce and diced some tomatoes and onion as well."

"It looks like you brought my favorite tortilla strips," Levi said about the chips poking out of one of the bags he was carrying as he walked into the cabin. "I'm hoping that means you brought salsa?"

"Some of Mom's homemade," Ellie assured him.

"I've got the tequila and limes for margaritas," Levi added.

I opened my freezer and took out a bag of ice. I missed Zak, but it was good to have the old gang together again.

"So how did Barbie take it when you told her you were hanging with us tonight?" Ellie asked.

"She wasn't happy," Levi admitted. "She doesn't really understand why I'd want to be friends with women I don't sleep with. She says it's unnatural to have close friends of the opposite sex."

"That's crazy," Ellie declared.

"Yeah. I think my relationship with the fabulous B may be coming to its natural conclusion. I really enjoyed being with her at first, but she seems to be obsessed with moving things to a more-committed level, and I don't think I'm ready for that."

Ellie smiled.

"I wouldn't wait too long if you're planning to end it. Valentine's Day is coming up, and everyone knows that ending a relationship within a week of the dance is considered to be a relationship faux pas," I pointed out.

"I hadn't thought of that. I guess I should really give it some thought. If I do break up with her, I'll need a date for the dance. You wanna be my backup?" Levi asked Ellie.

"Absolutely not."

"Why not?" Levi actually looked surprised. "We've gone together before."

"You seriously think I'd agree to go to the dance with you knowing that I'm only the backup in case things don't work out with Barbie?"

"Why not? That's what buds do. They have each other's back."

Ellie rolled her eyes. "Sometimes you can be so clueless. Besides, I'm going to the dance with Rob."

"It seems like you and Rob have been hanging out a lot lately," he said.

"I like Rob," Ellie responded. "He's fun, and our relationship is easy and uncomplicated."

"Sounds like a real yawner."

"My relationship with Rob is not a yawner," Ellie defended.

"I just call them like I see them." Levi shrugged.

If I didn't know better, I'd say Levi sounded more like a jealous boyfriend than an impartial friend. Perhaps, I decided, there was more to the Levi-and-Ellie thing than I'd originally thought.

"Barbie still pressuring you to move in with her?" I decided to change the subject before Ellie clobbered Levi with the frying pan in her hand.

"She's not backing off from the idea at all, in spite of the fact that I told her I really wasn't interested in doing something like that at this point. How about you? Do you and Zak have any plans to cohabitate?"

"Zak and I are taking things slow. I love being with him, but moving in is a huge step. I think we need to get used to being a couple and see how it goes."

"Right!" Levi agreed. "That's what I've been telling Barbie, but she thinks that three months of dating is more than enough time to know if things are going to work out or not."

"All this commitment talk is making my skin itch," I commented. "Let's open the tequila."

The thing about me is that once I'm in a committed relationship, I'm *all* in, and I don't like anyone or anything messing with the security that can be found in having things calm and steady. On the other hand, letting someone new in—I mean, really letting them in, to the point where they share my everyday life and have a piece of my heart—is something I've never been good at. Unless, of course, the *someone* in question has fur and four legs, and then I'm committed in a minute. I like Zak. I probably even love him. But there are things about him that give me pause, such as his tendency toward secrecy and his natural ability to cause any woman he comes into contact with to fall instantly in lust with him. Ellie has pointed out many times that it's natural for women to throw themselves at Zak; not only is he a total babe, but he's also ridiculously rich. To be honest, I sort of wish he wasn't.

Chapter 2

Monday, February 3

The next morning I was feeling the effects of the margaritas, the spicy food, and the late night, but I still managed to get up when the alarm went off so that I could meet Jeremy at the Zoo as planned. Normally, I'm not a huge fan of early morning meetings, but the county official who was assigned to inspect the improvements we'd made to the property insisted that the only time he was available to meet this week was first thing Monday morning. If we hadn't taken the appointment, which turned out to be a last-minute cancelation, we would have had to wait another four weeks for the reinspection of the few items he'd highlighted in his initial report. To be honest, jumping through all the hoops the county required to update the facility Zak had bought from them had turned out to be a nightmare I hadn't really anticipated. The end result was fabulous, but I was more than a little happy to be nearing the end of the road.

"You look terrible," Jeremy greeted me as he pulled into the parking lot at the same time I did. "Too much fun?"

"Something like that," I groaned as I began to regret scarfing down the second burrito, followed by a double serving of brownies and ice cream.

"Been there." Jeremy, a twenty-one-year-old, stick-thin heavy metal drummer with a nose ring and a neck tattoo, knew a thing or two about *too much fun.* "I think I have some antacids in my desk."

"Thanks." I waited while Charlie jumped down from the truck before retrieving the bags I'd stashed on the floor of the cab.

"You might want to splash a little water on your face before the inspector gets here," Jeremy suggested as I locked the door to the truck.

"That bad?"

"Oh, yeah."

I slung my purse over my shoulder and turned toward the building. "Isn't that Trent's truck?" I asked as I noticed the pickup belonging to one of the contractors working on our remodel parked near the back door. It was covered in snow, so it appeared to have been parked there all night.

"Yeah. I wonder why he left it."

"Maybe it wouldn't start, so he got a ride," I said hopefully. I suddenly began to get a queasy feeling in the pit of my stomach that had nothing to do with salsa and tequila.

"He did mention that he'd been having problems with it," Jeremy agreed.

The tension in my body lessened as I remembered that Trent *had* said something about the finicky ignition system. I suppose it could be all the murder and mayhem our little town has experienced in the past few months, but it seems that everywhere I looked, I saw murder and mayhem. "I'm kind of surprised he didn't call one of us to let us know he was leaving it."

Jeremy shrugged. "Maybe he planned to get here before we did. I hope he got everything working okay."

"He said he would," I responded. During his initial visit, the county inspector had noted that the electrical panel needed to be updated, and we'd been waiting for the correct supplies for over two weeks. They'd finally arrived yesterday so, knowing that Kevin was out of town on a ski trip and the inspector was returning today, Trent had offered to come by after he completed a plumbing job he was working on over the weekend.

"Guess we should check to make certain before the inspector gets here," Jeremy suggested. "It wouldn't look too good if he made the trip up the mountain before the repairs were completed."

I placed the bags I was carrying on my desk, then stashed my purse in the cabinet where I kept my personal possessions. I checked to see if the light on the answering machine was flashing before Charlie and I followed Jeremy down the hall.

"It seems the new equipment has been installed as promised, but it looks like Trent left his tools and supplies behind," Jeremy observed.

"Maybe he figured he'd get his stuff when he came back for the truck."

Jeremy flipped a few switches on the new panel. "The lights are working."

"How about the cameras in the wild-animal cages?"

Jeremy flipped a few more switches and then walked farther down the hall to check things out. He stopped in front of the newly built bear enclosure. I walked up behind him, then stopped dead in my tracks.

"Is that what I think it is?" I asked.

"Afraid so."

Two hours later, I sat with Jeremy in the waiting room of the sheriff's office, wondering what sort of evil curse had been cast that would cause me to be the one to find three dead bodies in three months. Especially since I happened to live in a town that, prior to this unusual set of circumstances, hadn't seen a murder in the past three decades. Ashton Falls is a charming, quiet, and peaceful town. Most folks didn't even lock their doors, and no one worried about walking around after dark or giving rides to strangers.

"I can't believe this is happening to me," I groaned.

"To you? What about Trent?" Jeremy pointed out.

"You have a point." Perhaps it was just a *bit* insensitive of me to be worrying more about the probable delay to our opening than the murder of a seemingly nice guy who had just been going about his business when someone broke in and ended his life. "I wonder who shot him?"

"I have no idea. The guy was fairly new to town and seemed to keep to himself. I can't imagine he's made any enemies in the short time he's been living in Ashton Falls. It looked like someone came in while he was working on the panel. If I had to guess, I'd say poor Trent was simply in the wrong place at the wrong time," Jeremy speculated.

"Yeah, but why would someone break into the Zoo? We aren't even open yet, and we certainly don't have anything of real value on the premises."

"That I don't know," Jeremy admitted. "Did you get hold of Zak?"

"Yeah. He's going to wrap things up and come home early, maybe even by tomorrow night. I think he's afraid I'm going to jump into the murder investigation and get myself arrested."

"Are you?" Jeremy asked. "Going to jump into the investigation?"

"Zak wants me to let Sheriff Salinger handle it."

"And are you going to?"

"Probably not."

"Zoe, the sheriff will see you now," the new receptionist informed me. She'd only lived in Ashton Falls for a few months, but we'd already come into contact with each other more often than I'd care to confess. "Sheriff Salinger asked that you leave Charlie with me until after your interview. Mr. Fisher, Sheriff Salinger would like you to speak to one of the deputies, if you don't mind."

"Sure, whatever gets me out of here the quickest," Jeremy answered.

"Zoe, you know where Salinger's office is." I couldn't help but feel that there was a bit of attitude behind that seemingly innocent statement. Could I help it if dead people kept finding me?

I hated to leave Charlie, but he seemed content to wait with the receptionist, so I showed myself down the hall and knocked on Sheriff Salinger's door. I opened it and entered when instructed to do so.

"We've really got to stop meeting this way," I teased as I sat down on the hard plastic chair on the other side of his desk. "What will people think?"

"Good question," Salinger agreed. "What will people think? Would you care to tell me where you were between five-thirty and seven-thirty last night?"

"Right to the point. I like that in a man."

Salinger apparently didn't appreciate my attempt at humor; he simply stared at me with steely eyes and waited for an answer.

"I was at home. At the boathouse, with Levi and Ellie. We had dinner, and they must have left around midnight."

"Would that be Levi Denton and Ellie Davis?"

I wanted to say *duh* but settled for *yes*. For those of you who may not be aware of my relationship with Sheriff Salinger, suffice it to say that it's a long and rather unpleasant one at best. You see, I have a tendency to butt into matters that are probably none of my business and, as a result, have at times gotten in the way of one official investigation or another. And while I'll admit that my meddling may have been of little to no help to the good man and his band of misfit deputies, it would seem that after I've identified not one but two killers in the past few months, the guy would give me a break and let bygones be bygones.

"Mr. Everett had a key to the Zoo on his person, which I assume is how he accessed the property. Can you tell me what he was doing there after hours?"

"Our electrical panel needed updating, and Trent had just gotten in some parts we'd been waiting for. He had a job yesterday, but his employer assured me he'd stop by afterward. He had a key, as do several of the contractors we've been working with."

"Do you know anyone else who might have come by last evening?" Salinger asked. "Another contractor, or an employee, perhaps?"

"Jeremy and I are the only employees and we weren't there. Zak is out of town, and the remodel is pretty much complete. No one other than Trent had any reason to be there."

"Did you notice anything missing?"

"You think Trent was the victim of a robbery gone bad?" I realized.

"It's a theory."

"I didn't notice anything missing, but to be honest, I didn't really look around. The only thing currently in the building that anyone might want to steal would be the veterinary supplies and Scott," I said, referring to the town vet, "keeps the medications and all his valuable equipment locked up in a metal cabinet in the exam room. I suppose we should check on it, though."

"I'll have one of my deputies meet the vet at the property. Can you think of any other reason someone might have broken in?"

"No, not a one."

"Okay, then can you think of anyone who might have a vendetta against you?"

"Other than you?" This time Salinger actually smiled. "Why do you ask? I wasn't even there."

"True, but the killer might have noticed the lights on and assumed you or perhaps your assistant were in the facility."

"I can't think of anyone I've annoyed enough to want to kill me," I answered.

"Prior to this morning, when were you last at the facility?"

"Saturday morning. That's when Jeremy, Levi, Ellie, and I finished the painting."

"And when was the last time you spoke to Mr. Everett?"

"Almost a week ago. Kevin Michaels is the actual contractor on the job. He called me yesterday morning and told me that he'd spoken to Trent, and the supplies for our panel had come in. He was out of town for the day, so he asked Trent to come by to install them. Kevin informed me that Trent had already committed to a plumbing job but would stop by when he was done with it."

"And you didn't arrange to meet him at the site?"

"No. Trent had a key, and he's been working with us for a couple of months, so I was comfortable with him being there on his own."

"Who else knew he'd be there last evening?"

"Just me and Jeremy."

Salinger made some notes. "You mentioned that you'd been working with the victim for a couple of months. Had he mentioned anyone he might be having a problem with? Ex-girlfriend? Angry customer?"

"No, no one. Trent is . . . I mean *was* a really nice guy. I can't imagine why anyone would want him dead."

Salinger made a few more notes and then sat back and looked at me. "Can you think of anything else? Maybe you want to share some of your Zoe insight?"

"Honestly, I wish I had some insight right now, but I'm afraid I really don't at the moment."

"Okay, then you can go for now. We'll call you if we have additional questions. The property is being cordoned off and the locks will be changed effective immediately. You'll be given keys when we've completed our investigation."

After leaving the sheriff's office, I drove past the Zoo. The entrance was taped and several official-looking vehicles were parked in the parking lot. I realized that this meant we wouldn't be opening on Thursday as planned, but I supposed there wasn't anything I could do there, so Charlie and I returned to the boathouse, where Levi and Ellie were waiting for me. If there's one thing you can say for my two best friends, it's that they're always there when I need them. I have no idea how they found out about the murder, but they had and were waiting to offer support before I even had to ask for it.

"Are you okay?" Levi asked as he and Ellie enveloped me in a giant group hug.

"Yeah, I'm fine." I relaxed into the emotional comfort.

"I overheard a couple of guys in the restaurant mention that the dead man lived in the area, but I'm pretty sure I've never met him," Ellie said after I took a step back.

"His name was Trent Everett. He was working for Kevin Michaels, which is how I met him. He seemed like a nice guy, although he sort of kept to himself. I'm pretty sure he only moved here a short while ago."

"Did the sheriff mention any suspects?" Levi asked as he poured me a glass of wine.

"Not to me. He did theorize that Trent might simply have gotten caught in a robbery gone bad."

"Poor guy," Ellie sympathized as we all settled onto the sofa in front of the fireplace. "I guess this puts the kibosh on your opening."

"Looks like it, unless Zak can pull some strings."

"So when is Zak supposed to be back?" Ellie asked.

"Late tomorrow evening or early on Wednesday. I figure I'll leave the door open in case he does make it tomorrow and decides to stop by."

"He doesn't have a key?" Ellie asked.

"No. I guess I never thought to give him one."

"Do you have a key to his place?" Levi asked.

"Yeah, but I sometimes water his plants when he's out of town."

"Girl, you need to give the man a key," Levi advised. "The balance of power is skewed otherwise."

"The balance of power?"

"Relationships are built on a very fragile balance of power," Levi explained. "If he gave you a key and you don't return the gesture, things are off balance, and your relationship is headed for problems."

"You're making that up," I challenged.

"Come on, Ellie, back me up."

"As much as I hate to admit it, I think Levi has a point. You should definitely give Zak a key. It will show him that you're as invested in the relationship as he is, which we all know is untrue, but at least you can put up a good front."

"What do you mean it's untrue?" I asked. "I'm invested in the relationship as much as Zak is."

Levi and Ellie looked at each other and shook their heads.

"I am," I insisted.

"Whatever you say, sweetie." I could tell Ellie was coddling me. "How about we get some food to go with this wine and tequila before we all end up with hangovers in the morning?"

"Pizza," Levi suggested.

"Pizza sounds good," Ellie agreed.

As we demolished two large pizzas, Levi, Ellie, and I discussed the murder and possible suspects. None of us knew Trent well enough to figure out who might want him dead, but we all agreed that a conversation with Kevin would be the best place to start. We momentarily discussed the idea of staying out of it and letting Salinger do his job, but I really wanted to get the Zoo open as soon as possible, and Salinger wasn't known for his speedy approach to solving crime.

"You realize that if Trent's death was actually the result of a robbery gone bad, it could have just as easily been you or Jeremy killed last night?" Ellie pointed out.

"Yeah, I thought of that. I have to admit the idea gives me the chills, but I honestly don't think Trent's death is the result of a robbery. We don't have anything stored at the facility worth killing for."

"So other than talking to Kevin, any idea how you're going to investigate a murder when there are no apparent clues and you didn't really know the victim all that well?" Levi wondered.

"Not really," I admitted. "Maybe the sheriff's guys will find some clues when they do their investigation. It's frustrating that I can't get in the Zoo to look around. I keep trying to remember whether I noticed anything out of place when Jeremy and I first got there this morning. The panel was fixed, but Trent's tools were still on the floor. I assume whomever came in did so just as Trent was finishing up. I did find it a little odd that his body was found down the hall, in the bear cage. I've been trying to figure out why the killer didn't just shoot him in the hall, where he was working."

"Maybe Trent heard someone come in and went down the hall to try to hide," Ellie speculated.

"Maybe, but it seems like if Trent heard footsteps or the door slam, he would just have assumed it was Jeremy or me. Why hide?"

"Maybe he saw whomever it was that came in and was afraid of them."

"Indicating that he knew his killer," I realized.

"It's a theory." Ellie shrugged.

"So if Trent was trying to hide, or possibly escape through one of the rear exits, then he must have known the killer and realized he was in danger. If that's true, Salinger's robbery theory goes out of the window."

"Okay, so who would want Trent dead?" Levi asked.

"I don't have a clue."

Chapter 3

Tuesday, February 4

By the time Charlie and I unwrapped ourselves from our heavy down comforter the next morning, it was snowing a bit harder than it had been the previous day. I pulled on my heavy slippers and we made our way downstairs to start the coffee and light the fire. I stood at the back window, which overlooks the lake, enjoying the view as I sipped my first cup of liquid adrenaline. Large snowflakes drifted from dark clouds, dancing on air currents, until they landed softly on the dark lake, melting on impact and merging with the large body of water. I loved the solitude and the sound of silence on dark and stormy days. The snow had begun to accumulate on the beach, and I knew the deck and walkway wouldn't be far behind.

I finished my coffee and headed upstairs to shower and dress. Heavy jeans, thick wool socks, a heavy wool sweater layered over a cotton turtleneck, knee-high boots, and a down jacket should keep me warm in the subfreezing temperatures predicted for the day. After we took a quick shovel to the deck and walkway, we planned to stop off at Rosie's for some much-deserved nourishment, but Ellie called and asked me to meet her at a little shop on the pier. She'd been trying to buy it since the previous fall.

"You got it?" I guessed as Charlie and I walked into the run-down little shop where Ellie was waiting for us.

"I got it," she confirmed.

"Congratulations," I said, hugging my best friend.

"I'm so excited," Ellie shared. "With all the hoops Blakely made us jump through, I didn't think we'd ever get this far."

Blakely is the bank president and keeper of the funds Ellie and her mom, Rosie, needed to make their dream come true.

"I'm so happy for you. So have you figured out a name? Rosie's on the Pier, or maybe the more mundane Rosie's Two?"

"Actually," Ellie beamed, "Mom suggested we call it Ellie's."

"Really?" I smiled. "That's wonderful."

"We talked about it, and she thinks I'm ready to run my own place, so she's going to let me run Ellie's while she continues to run Rosie's. She's even going to let me decorate it any way I like."

I looked around the little shop. It had one of the best locations in town, but the interior needed a major facelift if it was going to provide the quintessential small-town feel that Rosie's did. The facility wasn't large enough to house an industrial kitchen, so Ellie's idea was to sell sandwiches, salads, and soup premade in Rosie's main kitchen to the crowd who gathered at the lake during the warm summer months. There was a large deck area where they planned to set up an outdoor patio, as well as several BBQs where they could grill ribs, chicken, and hamburgers made to order. During the winter, when the beach crowd had migrated indoors and the cross- country ski mob overran the beach, they planned to convert the sandwich and BBQ shop into a warming hut specializing in hot beverages, both with and without alcohol, as well as homemade soup, bread, muffins, and other sweet treats.

"Have you decided how you're going to decorate?" I asked.

"Not totally," Ellie admitted. "The place is too small to pull off all the props built into Rosie's." Rosie's is decorated with an eclectic assortment of skis, sleds, snowshoes, fishing poles, climbing ropes, and other antiques that define the area. "I was thinking I'd paint the walls a light color, perhaps a creamy white or pale yellow. Something to make the space feel larger."

"Once you decide, I'm in on helping with the painting," I offered. Both Levi and Ellie had put in tons of hours during the remodel of the Zoo. Helping Ellie with her project was the least I could do.

I wandered over to the wall of windows at the back of the building. The shop had been built on the edge of the pier, so when you looked out of the back windows, you looked directly out at the water.

"I thought I'd put in a counter along the back wall, where people can sit and look out at the lake. I'd love to have a real wood fireplace like Rosie's, but given the lack of space, I've pretty much decided to settle for a small gas unit over there in the corner. I'm going to put sofas and a coffee table surrounding it, where people can warm up and have a drink when they come in from skiing."

"You might want to put some of those portable fireplaces on the deck," I suggested. "The bar at the ski resort has outdoor seating in the winter and it's always packed except for the stormiest of days."

"That's a great idea," Ellie said. "This has taken so long to make happen, but now that I've actually been handed the key, I feel like there's so much to do and so little time. I need to remodel the place, come up with a menu, apply for a liquor license, and get my county permits."

"Don't worry. I'll help," I assured her. "And I'm sure Zak and Levi will as well. It's going to be fantastic."

"It is, isn't it?" Ellie beamed. "At first I wasn't sure it would work, since the shop doesn't have a kitchen, but the more I thought about it, the more certain I was that simple food provided in disposable containers was exactly what the customers who hang out at the beach would embrace."

"I think you're right. And there's plenty of room on that back counter for a microwave, a toaster oven, and slow cookers. You could even do hot sandwiches like meatballs, pulled pork, and shredded BBQ beef. Dang, now I'm hungry."

"We'll have to go back to Rosie's for sustenance. I should get back anyway, but when Blakely called this morning to tell me the paperwork was complete and the escrow closed, I just had to come over."

"I don't blame you. The place is going to be awesome."

"By the way," Ellie shared as she began shutting off lights and locking up, "Pack Rat Nelson came by Rosie's this morning." Pack Rat, so nicknamed due to his propensity for collecting *everything*, lived in a run-down cabin outside of town, but he spent much of every day in the alley behind the shops on Main

Street, collecting treasures from the garbage. "I usually give him old bread and pastries, so he stops by the back door every few days," Ellie explained. "Anyway, he wanted me to tell you that he was going through the Dumpsters behind the Zoo the other night while Trent was there. He said they spoke for a moment before Trent went inside to work."

"Did he see who else came by?" I asked excitedly. While the Zoo isn't on Main Street and therefore isn't part of Pack Rat's normal scavenging territory, I knew he'd been coming by since we'd been discarding materials associated with the remodel.

"Actually, he did. He said he saw three people come by, but he wouldn't tell me who they were. He wants you to stop by his cabin."

I looked at my watch. It was almost noon. "I'll go now," I decided. "If I have a chance, I'll stop by Rosie's after I talk to him."

"Okay, I'll catch up with you later."

Pack Rat Nelson lived in a three-room cabin that was packed with so many *treasures* you could barely get a body in the front door. Personally, I can't imagine living like that, but I don't think there's a single item in his too-cluttered life he would consider parting with. The large yard leading up to the cabin is as cluttered as the interior. I know the county has tried on more than one occasion to persuade Pack Rat to clean up his mess, but he maintains that his treasures are art and therefore not subject to the county's litter-control policies. I have to admit he does tend to display his wares in a creative way, and as far as I can tell, he doesn't leave out anything that might attract wildlife or present a fire danger.

"Zoe, I'm so glad you could stop by. Care to come in?"

I glanced at the tight space behind the man with bloodshot eyes and a bulbous nose. The house wasn't exactly dirty, but it was so cluttered with treasures that I doubted there was a single space big enough for both of us to stand. "Thanks, but it might be better to just talk on the porch. I left Charlie in the truck," I nodded behind me, "and I'd like to keep an eye on him."

"Sure makes sense." Pack Rat stepped out onto the covered deck, closing the door behind him.

"Ellie tells me that you were at the Zoo the night Trent Everett was killed." I decided that due to the cold temps and Pack Rat's thin shirt and pants, it was best to jump right in.

"I might have been."

I offered Pack Rat a $20 bill. "It's really important that you try to remember anything you saw."

"It was late. Already almost dark," Pack Rat qualified. "But I noticed that young electrician you've been working with arrived just as I was about to pack up and leave, so I stopped by to say hi. I'd spoken to him on other occasions, and he promised to save me any wiring scraps he might have. I wanted to see if he had any to donate that night."

"And did he?"

"Four green wires and three red." Pack Rat's eyes lit up like he'd just won the lottery.

"Was there anyone with him?" I asked.

"Not while I was talking to him, but a couple of folks came by while he was working inside."

"You stayed around after Trent went inside to work?"

"I wanted to dig through the scraps the sheet-rock guys left," Pack Rat explained.

"Do you remember who came by?"

Pack Rat glanced toward my truck. "My memory has been a little fuzzy this morning."

"I don't have any more cash," I informed him.

"That a flashlight on your dashboard?"

I turned and looked back toward the truck. The yellow flashlight I kept for emergencies was clearly displayed in the windshield. "Batteries are dead."

"Don't need batteries," Pack Rat informed me.

"Okay, I'll give you the flashlight if you have any information that can help me find Trent's killer."

"First one to stop by was that lady from the county. The one with the short curly hair who usually wears those long dresses with the heavy black shoes."

"Willa Walton?"

"Yeah, that sounds right."

"She drives a white Subaru," I clarified.

"That'd be her."

"How long did she stay?"

"'Bout fifteen minutes."

I realized that if Willa visited first, she couldn't have been the killer, but I supposed it made sense to talk with her to see what, if anything, she might know. "What time did she get there?"

"I guess about six."

"Did she bring anything with her?"

"She had a brown bag," Pack Rat provided. "The kind you'd pack a lunch in."

"Did you notice or hear anything else?"

"No." Pack Rat shook his head. "She drove into the lot, parked her car, and took the bag from the backseat. She went inside and came out a while later."

Most people looked at Pack Rat and the way he lived and assumed he was mentally limited, but I'd learned a long time ago that in spite of his strange hobby, he was both intelligent and observant.

"Okay, who else came by?"

"That woman with the long blond hair and much too short skirts who runs the child care."

"Tawny Upton?"

"Sounds right."

"And she came after Willa left?"

"'Bout twenty minutes after."

"How long did she stay?"

Pack Rat thought about it. "Not long. Maybe ten or fifteen minutes."

"Did she bring anything in with her?"

"She had her purse, but I didn't see nothin' else."

"And the third visitor?"

"Man I didn't recognize. Pretty sure he's from out of the area."

"Did he have anything with him?"

"Not that I noticed."

"Did you get a good enough look to describe him?"

"Tall, broad shoulders. Dark hair, dark shirt and pants, with a black wool jacket over the top. Would like to find myself a jacket like that. Looked like it would be warm, and might likely hold up for a bit."

"Did you hear anything?" Trent was shot. If the third visitor was the killer, it seemed Pack Rat would have heard a gunshot.

"Nope."

"Were you still there when the man left?"

"No. He stayed a while, and it was dark. I decided to head home. If I'd known . . ."

"Yeah, I know." I placed my hand on Pack Rat's filthy arm. I could tell he felt bad that he hadn't stuck around. "There probably wasn't much you could have done to help Trent anyway."

"Maybe. Maybe not."

"Well, thanks for sharing. If you want to follow me to my truck, we can see about that flashlight."

I figured that Willa would most likely still be at work in the county offices, so I decided to stop by there first. While Bryton Lake is the county seat and houses most of the county officials, Ashton Falls has a small facility that is shared by local officials and law enforcement. Willa works in the finance and records department and normally could be found at a desk behind the reception counter. She not only serves as one of the county's only full-time employees stationed in Ashton Falls but also as the chairperson for the events committee, on which I serve.

"Afternoon, Willa," I greeted her. Willa is a petite brunette in her midforties, though her sophisticated nature makes her seem much older. She's an exemplary employee and loyal friend and neighbor. She lives alone and, as far as I knew, never married or had children.

"Zoe, so nice to see you. Where's Charlie?"

"Waiting in the truck. I figured I'd only be a minute. I wanted to ask you about Trent Everett."

"Come in." Willa motioned me to come inside and indicated I should take a seat. "Trent was such a nice young man. It's such a shame about what happened."

I could see Willa was fighting an obviously strong emotion despite the casualness of her words. "You visited him at the Zoo the night he was killed."

"I did," she choked out. "He was supposed to come by my place for dinner, but he called to say he had to cancel because there was an emergency job you needed done. I had plenty of meat loaf, so I took him a sandwich and some of my homemade soup."

"You're friends?"

"He rented a room from me when he first moved to town." Willa paused as she wiped away a tear. "He's since gotten his own place, but he still comes by once a week or so to share a meal."

"Do you know anything about his past?"

Willa took a perfectly pressed white hankie from her cardigan pocket and gently dabbed at the tear forming in the corner of her eye. "No, not really. He mentioned being from the East Coast and having family in both New York and Florida. He seemed to really miss them, especially his grandmother. I think that's why we bonded the way we did. He said my cooking reminded him of a better and simpler time."

"But he never said why he moved to Ashton Falls?"

"No. He did mention some trouble in the past but didn't elaborate. I sort of got the impression that he fell in with a rough crowd when he was younger."

"Do you remember what time it was when you took Trent his supper?"

"'Bout six."

"Did you tell Salinger this?"

"Certainly. Is there a problem with my being at the Zoo?"

"No, not at all. You know you're welcome anytime."

"You're investigating," Willa accused. "I should have realized there was a reason for all the questions."

"I'm not," I said, defending myself.

"I specifically heard that Salinger told you to stay out of it and you promised you would." Willa glared at me in such a way as to make me feel like I'd been caught with my hand in the cookie jar.

"I'm out. Really." I held up my hands. "I spoke to Pack Rat, who saw you go in, and I was just curious whether you noticed anything out of the ordinary."

"I didn't, and *we* didn't have this conversation. I like you, Zoe, you know I do, but I work for the county. If you're participating in activities that Commissioner Cromwell or Sheriff Salinger wouldn't approve of, I don't want to know."

"Okay, I'm gone. And Willa . . ."

"Yes?"

"Thanks."

"Don't thank me unless you're going to take my advice and stay out of it."

"Okay. Have a good afternoon."

I momentarily considered taking Willa's advice, but, well, after all, I *am* Zoe, and even I have to admit that quitting when I still had one lead to check out would be a very un-Zoelike thing to do. I didn't know who the man was, but it wouldn't take any time at all to have a chat with Tawny, a single mom, who ran the local preschool and is also an event-committee member. It was still several hours before she would close for the day and I considered waiting to track her down at home but decided to stop by the facility to get a feel for things. If Tawny was busy with the kids, I'd just say hi and leave, but if she was working at her desk, I'd find out what I could about her relationship with Trent.

The Over the Rainbow Preschool is a brightly painted building with a large play area in the center of town. I knew Tawny had decided to open the center after her husband left her so she could both earn a living and spend time with her young children. The preschool and afterschool day-care facility was a huge hit with busy parents in the area because Tawny and her staff were both creative and disciplined in their approach. Luckily, it was nap time, and Tawny was eating a sandwich in the break room when I arrived.

"I thought you might be by." She glanced up at me as I walked through the door.

"Really?" I tried to appear innocent.

"I heard about Trent. I figured it was only a matter of time before you found out I was one of the last people to see him alive and came by to talk to me about it. To be honest, I'm surprised it took you this long. Tuna fish?" She pointed at a stack of sandwich halves.

"If you have extra." I really was starving by this point.

"Where's Charlie?"

"In the truck."

"Nap time is about over. Bring him in and I'll have my assistant supervise while he plays with the kids so that we can talk."

I returned to the truck and brought a very excited Charlie inside. Charlie adores playing with the kids. He's gentle and patient in spite of the fact that some of the younger kids haven't been taught how to play with a real-live animal and at times take all sorts of malevolent glee in pulling his ears and trying to poke him in the eye. Normally, I try to be there to supervise to ensure that the little ones don't actually injure him, but Tawny's assistant assured me she'd keep a close eye on things. By the time I returned to the break room, Tawny had poured me a glass of milk to go with my sandwich.

"Trent sometimes helps me out with projects I have going on at the preschool," Tawny jumped right in before I could even ask her a question. "I don't have extra money, so Trent pretty much does the work for cost. We try to keep it quiet because part of Trent's agreement with Kevin is that he isn't supposed to moonlight. We had been discussing a room addition so that I can accommodate additional infants in the hope of turning an actual profit, and he'd e-mailed me the plans earlier in the day. I wanted to discuss a few things with him, so he suggested I stop by the Zoo so we could chat while he fixed your electrical panel."

Tawny paused to catch her breath. I could tell that, like Willa, she was suppressing an emotion she didn't want to share.

"He was fine when I stopped by. He mentioned that Willa had been by and brought him a meat-loaf sandwich, which he planned to enjoy once he finished the work he'd promised to do for you. He appeared to be all but done by the time we spoke. I think I arrived at about six-thirty and probably left fifteen minutes later."

"Did you tell Salinger all of this?"

"He hasn't asked."

"Did Trent ever mention any enemies?" I wondered. "Anyone who might want to do him harm?"

Tawny paused. "I've asked myself that question a hundred times since I found out what happened. Trent was such a nice guy. He was quiet and kept to himself. I can't imagine anyone wanting to hurt him, although he did let it slip one time that he used to hang out with a rough crowd that had gotten him into a lot of trouble. He didn't clarify what sort of trouble he'd gotten into, but I got the feeling it was something pretty serious. He seemed to have regretted his behavior in his earlier life and was committed to starting over and making a success of himself."

"How did you meet him?"

"I had a circuit breaker that kept blowing. It created a real problem because it controlled all the lights for the facility, among other things. I called Kevin to take a look at it and he sent Trent. When Trent told me I was going to need all new wiring, I broke into tears. The profit margin for the preschool is pretty much nonexistent. Owning it allows me to pay my bills and be available for my own kids but little more. When I told Trent there was no way I could afford all new wiring, he volunteered to do it for cost. Technically, he cut Kevin out of a potential profit that we figured wouldn't have gone over well, so we agreed Trent would do it on his own time, after hours."

I couldn't help but wonder if Trent made a regular habit of cutting out Kevin, and perhaps he'd found out about it. Seemed like as good a reason as any for murder, and Kevin knew where Trent was headed that night.

"Do you know if Trent did special deals for anyone else?" I asked.

"Not that I know of, although he did mention that he was planning to help Mary Grayson out with a plumbing issue."

I know Mary, a widow with four kids, and she wouldn't have any more money than Tawny to fix her plumbing.

"If you think of anything else, please call me."

"I will," Tawny promised. "Lord knows Salinger isn't going to find out who killed Trent, and he deserves to have justice for his death. He was a good man and I'm really going to miss him."

I thought about talking to Mary, but her kids would be out of school by this time of day. She might have something to share, but Pack Rat had indicated that Trent's third visitor was a man, and my money was on him as the killer. I called Kevin's office line, but his wife told me he was off the mountain picking up supplies and wouldn't be available to return my call until the next day. I looked at my watch. Levi would be off work in less than an hour, and Rosie's had closed ten minutes earlier. I texted both of my best friends to ask if they wanted to meet for a drink. We agreed on four-thirty, which gave me time to take Charlie home and clean up a bit.

Mulligan's Bar and Grill isn't known for its food, yet it remains a favorite of long-time residents of Ashton Falls. It's the type of place you go if you want to sit in your favorite booth with your best friend and eat comfort food. After we'd placed our order, Ellie launched into her seemingly rehearsed speech about the ideas she had for her new sandwich shop.

"Maybe we can build a bench all the way around the fireplace on the back wall," Levi suggested. "I'm thinking a portable unit of some type that you can use in the winter and remove during the summer."

"Zoe already suggested outdoor seating in the winter," Ellie informed him, "and I'd already thought of the bench. Got any other ideas?"

"A beer cave."

"A beer cave?" Ellie asked. "I don't have a lot of room."

"I noticed a large storage room off the wall on the east side of the room while I was checking the place out. Right now access is from the outside, but it would be easy enough to close that off and create a door from the inside. You'd need to upgrade the insulation and provide refrigeration, but it would be an awesome attraction that would draw in a happy-hour crowd."

"I don't know." Ellie frowned. "I'm not sure the beer-cave crowd is the clientele I'm looking for, but I like the idea of creating additional interior space by accessing the storage area. I hadn't even thought of that. Will you help me with the remodel?" Ellie asked.

"I'd love to. We can start on Saturday."

I couldn't help but feel that Ellie's huge smile had more to do with *who* would be building her extra room than the room itself.

"Any progress on your investigation?" Ellie asked.

"Yes and no," I said. I explained about the three people Pack Rat had seen go into the Zoo that night. I shared my conversation with Willa and Tawny, and we all agreed that the third visitor had to be our prime suspect. Ellie and Levi both expressed their regret that they'd never gotten to know Trent after learning about his Good Samaritan deeds.

"So how about you?" Ellie looked at Levi. "Anything new in your life?"

"Since yesterday?" Levi laughed.

"Yeah, I guess we have been hanging out a lot this week. How's Barbie taking it?"

"Barbie and I aren't talking at the moment," Levi admitted. "I've pretty much decided to break if off with her, but every time I mention to her that we need to have a talk, she makes up some excuse as to why we can't meet."

"So don't call ahead," Ellie suggested. "Just show up at her house and do it quick. I'm sure she realizes this is coming, which is most likely why she's been avoiding you. You'll both feel better after you put this behind you."

"I'm sure you're right. How are things going with Rob?"

"Good. We're going out tomorrow night."

I sat quietly and watched my best friends as they discussed their love lives. At first I had been horrified by the idea that Ellie might have feelings of the romantic kind for Levi, but as I watched them, I decided that a relationship between the two could be just about right. Of course, they seemed to be on different pages. First Levi was dating Barbie, and now that he'd pretty much decided to end that relationship, Ellie was just beginning one with Rob. I decided that if Levi and Ellie were meant to be together, the universe would have to provide the opportunity, as it had for Zak and me.

After I got home, I straightened up in anticipation of Zak's arrival. He hadn't exactly said he *would* stop by, but it had been several days and I was certain he was as anxious to see me as I was to see him. I threw another log on the fire, softened the lighting, lowered the volume on the stereo, and sat looking out at the lake with Charlie curled up next to me, Spade in my lap, and Marlow on the back of the sofa near my head. I couldn't help but wonder if Ellie wasn't onto something when she indicated—okay, flat-out stated—that Zak was more committed to our relationship than I was. I felt committed. At least I thought I did. I certainly felt jealousy where Zak was concerned, but were jealousy and commitment the same thing? Maybe Ellie was right. Maybe Zak was more invested than I was and I simply hadn't noticed.

In my twenty-four years, I'd had several casual relationships, but never anything as serious as what I'd like to have with Zak. Perhaps I really didn't understand the rules of the game. Zak never said anything about a key, and he'd never once indicated he was in any way dissatisfied with the rate at which our relationship was developing, but Ellie wasn't wrong when she indicated that he'd made more concessions to our partnership than I had. I thought about the million and one things Zak had done for me over the past few months and felt terrible that I hadn't done more.

I must have fallen asleep at some point because the next thing I knew, I was laying on the couch between three warm bodies—Charlie and the cats—and someone was kissing my neck.

"Zak," I moaned without opening my eyes. It was possible I was dreaming, and if I was, I didn't want to wake up.

"I leave for a couple of days and the next thing I know, you're knee deep in dead bodies," Zak teased.

The delicious feel of Zak's lips working their way from my neck to my mouth caused a tingling sensation up my spine. I wrapped my arms around his neck and melted into his body as he carried me up the stairs to my bedroom.

Chapter 4

Wednesday, February 5

Much to my disappointment, Zak was gone when I woke up the next morning. He'd left a note, telling me that he was going to be tied up all day but that he planned to have a discussion with both the sheriff and the county about opening the Zoo the following day, as planned. He asked me to let him handle things and not to make matters worse by digging around in the case. Although it goes against my nature to do so, I decided to honor Zak's request, at least for the time being, and go about my day as if I hadn't just found a body in my bear cage and everything I'd worked so hard for over the past few months wasn't once again going to be delayed indefinitely.

I was proud of my decision to leave the investigation in the hands of the professionals . . . for about two minutes. And then I remembered everything I'd learned about Trent the previous day. While he'd always been friendly and cordial while working on the remodel at the Zoo, I'd never really stopped to talk to him, and he'd never really opened the door for me to do so. Suddenly, I felt bad for treating the guy, who obviously had a warm and giving heart, like a distant acquaintance. The more I thought about it, the more I realized that Jeremy must have chatted with Trent on more than a casual basis; he was the type to start a conversation with *everyone* with whom he came into contact. The Zoo was still off-limits, so I called Jeremy and offered to take him to lunch.

After taking Charlie for a run and topping off the cats' food and water, I got dressed in warm winter clothes and set off for town. I'd called ahead and informed Ellie that I hoped to have a private conversation with Jeremy, so she'd saved us the table in the back of Rosie's.

"So what's up?" Jeremy asked as Ellie headed back to the kitchen with our order.

"I was interested in finding out what you knew about Trent," I began. "I know the two of you spent a lot of time together over the past couple of months."

"I'm not sure what I can tell you." Jeremy stirred at least ten packets of sugar into his iced tea, which I am fairly certain he drinks every one of the 365 days of the year. "He was a nice guy. Quiet. Lived in town but kept to himself. Seemed to work a lot. He frequently mentioned side jobs he did in the evening, after finishing with Kevin for the day."

"Can you think of any side jobs in particular?" I asked as Jeremy tasted his drink and then added two more packets of sugar.

"I know he was helping Tawny with the preschool, and I remember him mentioning something about helping Old Man Johnson with some insulation."

Old Man Johnson lives in a small cabin just outside of town. It had to be at least fifty years old, and the draft through the cracks on the log siding created temperatures resembling an icebox in the middle of winter. Old Man Johnson had lived in Ashton Falls as long as anyone could remember. He was a crusty sort who didn't have a lot of use for people but loved animals. He'd adopted several dogs from the shelter over the years, and I felt that he and I were on good-enough terms that he'd talk to me. Maybe.

"Anything else? Did he ever mention a girlfriend or a group he socialized with?"

"Not that I can remember. It seemed to me like he worked most of the time, although he did say something about needing to leave early one of the times he was at the Zoo because he was going to dinner at someone's house. I don't remember him mentioning whose house it was, but he mentioned he was looking forward to enjoying the type of food he'd eaten when he was growing up."

"Did he happen to tell you where he lived before this?"

Jeremy thought about it. "Not specifically, but he talked about Piazza's Pizza all the time."

"Piazza's Pizza?" I'd never heard of the place.

"It's a small, family-owned pizza place in the Bronx. I only know about it because I have a cousin who lives in New York and he's always saying that Piazza's has the best pizza he's ever tasted. One day Trent mentioned it in passing, and I told him that I'd heard of the place, and he went into a lengthy discussion about the thickness of the sauce, the crispness of the crust, and the five cheeses that are used to make that epicurean delight. My guess is that Trent either lived in the area or spent a significant amount of time there at some point."

"Anything else you can think of?" I asked as Ellie brought our food.

Jeremy took a bite of his sandwich. He chewed loudly as he considered my question. I handed him a napkin to wipe the mayo off his chin. Although Jeremy is only a few years younger than me, there were times when I felt like he was the child and I was the adult.

"Trent mentioned his grandmother on more than one occasion," Jeremy said, once he'd swallowed. "He never said so directly, but I got the idea that he and his sister were raised in a family with minimal parental influence other than the times they visited their grandparents, who lived some distance away."

"Sister?"

"Yeah. He never mentioned her name, but he said things like *we'd* really look forward to those summer visits. One day I asked about siblings, and he said he had an older sister."

"I suppose I should mention this to Salinger. I'm sure he's looking for next of kin to notify."

After lunch, I decided to call on Old Man Johnson. The drive to his cabin took only minutes. By the time I arrived, I wished I had Charlie with me as an ice breaker. At least the five dogs that greeted me as I pulled into the drive remembered me. I got down from my truck and said hello to Johnson's pack before treading carefully over the icy walkway to the front door.

"Mr. Johnson," I called as I knocked loudly. "It's Zoe Donovan." Old Man Johnson was deaf in one ear, so I hoped he'd heard me. It was cold and windy, and I didn't relish standing outside on the stoop longer than I had to.

"Mr. Johnson." I knocked again.

"Hang on a minute." I heard something crash, followed by a scuffle, and, eventually, footsteps heading toward the door.

I smiled when the man opened the door dressed in nothing but bright red long johns. "Did I wake you?"

"Humph," he groaned. "What can I do for you?"

"I wanted to ask about Trent Everett, if you have a minute."

"Yeah, okay," he said, opening the door wider, "come on in."

The cabin was cozy, well kept, and surprisingly warm.

"Have a seat." Johnson pointed toward the worn but comfortable-looking sofa. "I'll just get some pants on and join you."

I looked around the room while I waited. Johnson had an entire wall plastered with photographs of the area taken long before I was born. It was interesting to see empty lots where buildings now stood, and old structures that had been torn down to make way for new ones. Johnson had a photo of Donovan's, the store my dad now owned and my pappy had built, before the addition. The photos Johnson had should really be on public display. Perhaps I'd have someone approach him about the idea. At another time. Today, Trent Everett was the main topic on my mind.

"So you wanted to talk?" Johnson asked when he returned to the room wearing worn jeans over his long johns.

"I heard that Trent helped you out with some insulation, and by the nice and toasty feel of the place, I assume he completed the job."

"Yeah, so?"

"I'm trying to figure out who might have killed him."

"You think I did?"

"No, not at all," I quickly assured him. "I just figured the two of you might have talked while he was here. Maybe you have some insight as to who might have wanted him dead."

Johnson rubbed his chin, which was covered with stubble, as he thought about it. "We chatted a bit. Shared my stew with him a time or two. Can't recall him mentioning anyone who had a beef with him. He was a real nice kid. Can't imagine anyone wanting to hurt him."

"How exactly did you meet him?"

"Willa Walton sent him around. She'd been by to ask about my tree-cutting permit and noticed how cold it was inside. Boy did a real nice job, and it didn't cost me a penny."

"He didn't charge you *anything*?"

"Nope. Said I reminded him of his grandpa and he was happy to help out."

It seemed strange to me that a man who was as attached to his family as Trent seemed to be would move to a place where he didn't know anyone. I had to wonder if there was a reason for his departure from the place where he'd grown up.

"Did Trent ever tell you anything about his grandparents, or anything else for that matter, about his past?"

"Not a lot. Guess his mom grew up poor but married into some sort of rich and powerful family. It sounded like he didn't really get on with either of his parents or his dad's family, but he would go to stay with his mother's parents every summer. Seems like they lived on a farm in upstate New York. I think when he got older the visits stopped, but he mentioned a time or two that those summers were the best times of his life."

"Did he ever mention a sister?"

"Mentioned someone he referred to as Reenie."

"Reenie?"

"I got the feeling it was some sort of nickname for a close friend or maybe a sibling. He never elaborated and I never asked."

"Did he ever mention where he lived or what he did for a living prior to moving to Ashton Falls?"

"Can't say that he did. Other than stories about his grandparents and the farm, he didn't say much at all about his past."

"Okay, well, thank you for your time. I've enjoyed looking at your photos. I especially love this one of the store my pappy built."

"Your pappy is a good man. I remember when he first moved to this area. There weren't much of a town back then. Most folks came for the summer but returned to their homes in the valley once the first hint of snow was in the air. Your pappy cut and milled those logs himself. Took him a couple of years, but he built himself a right nice place."

"So you knew Pappy before he married my grandma?"

"I did. Never seen a man fall so hard or so fast as he did for that little spitfire who made it her business to tell him what for."

I smiled. "She did have spunk."

"Real looker too. Might have tried taking her for a spin myself, but your pappy had a ring on her finger quicker than you can say lickety-split."

"He's always told me it was love at first sight."

It occurred to me that my dad had told me the same thing about the first time he met my mom, although that hadn't worked out quite so well. If Zak was indeed my one true love—and it was a bit early to determine that—the family tradition would be broken with me. The first time I met Zak, the golden boy of Ashton Falls, I wanted to tear his eyes out. That thought gave me pause. Maybe love was supposed to be instantaneous. Maybe what I had with Zak wasn't love at all. . . .

"Heard you're opening the shelter back up."

"Yeah, tomorrow, I hope."

"Been thinking about another dog. Grover is getting old and Tumbler is going blind. Might want to take on a younger dog I can train to hunt."

"If we get in a dog that I think will work out, I'll call you."

"Appreciate that."

After leaving Johnson's, I headed back toward town. I was learning a lot about the man Trent had been since moving to Ashton Falls, but not much about who he was prior to that. Maybe Zak could do a background search if he finished his other projects on time, and there was always the slim chance that Salinger would turn something up. In the meantime, I figured I'd have a chat with Mary Grayson. But first I'd stop by the boathouse and pick up Charlie. Mary loved Charlie and would welcome a visit.

I pulled into my drive and was delighted to see Zak's truck was parked near my front door. I hadn't yet given him a key, but I rarely locked my door except at night. It seemed odd that Zak would come by without calling first, but I supposed our relationship had moved beyond the formalities normally associated with being neighbors.

"You're leaving," I complained as we passed at the front door. "But I just got here. Can you stay for a while?"

"Sorry." Zak gave me a quick peck on the lips. "I've got to run. I couldn't find my phone, and I thought I might have left it here."

"You haven't had your phone all day?" The idea that Zak had left his phone at my place wasn't odd; the fact that it was hours since he'd left and was just noticing seemed a bit more suspect.

"I was working at home and didn't notice until I got ready to leave. I looked around, but it wasn't anywhere I could find it. After thinking about it, it occurred to me it might be in the pocket of the jacket I had on last night. I'm going to head back home and take another look."

"Do you have time for some lunch?" I tried for my most seductive voice, but he merely kissed me on the nose and said he didn't. He promised to call me later and left as abruptly as he must have arrived.

"Did you see that?" I asked Charlie. "I'm not sure I've ever felt quite so dismissed."

I'm sure if Charlie could talk, he'd remind me that not only had Zak had to cut his business trip short but he was also busy trying to get the Zoo open by the next day. He'd remind me that Zak loved me and most likely didn't intend to be abrupt, and that I should cut him some slack and get on with my day. If Charlie *had* said that, I might have listened, but instead I found myself sinking into an emotional slump it would take a crane to pull me out of.

Mary lived in a two-story house two blocks behind Main Street. The homes in the area were some of the first built in Ashton Falls, and while many of them were run-down, Mary kept hers as well as her limited funds would allow. Tawny had indicated that Trent had helped her out with a plumbing problem. It seemed our part-time contractor's assistant was well versed in many aspects of the construction industry. I couldn't help but wonder why he was working for what most likely barely topped minimum wage when he obviously had the skills to obtain a union job in a bigger town.

"Zoe," Mary greeted me as I walked up the front path, "and Charlie. What a nice surprise. Please do come in."

I wiped my feet on the front mat and checked Charlie's paws for mud before we entered the spotlessly clean if somewhat cluttered house.

"Can I get you some coffee? Perhaps a freshly baked muffin?"

"Thanks, but we can only stay for a few minutes."

"What can I do for you?" Mary asked as we settled onto the sofa in the living room.

"I wanted to ask you about Trent Everett."

My conversation with Mary started off much like the others had, with me asking questions about how she'd met Trent and her gushing about how he'd saved her from being homeless when he fixed her plumbing for free. Then I asked about any enemies he might have had, and she swore he was the kindest man to ever grace the earth. Toward the end of our chat, when I was asking about his life before he'd arrived in Ashton Falls, she got a distant look on her face.

"There was something," she shared. "He got a call while he was here. He went into the other room to take it, but these walls are thin and I couldn't help but overhear. It seemed he was speaking to a man by the name of Bruno. I didn't hear everything that was said, but Trent was upset that this Bruno had talked to someone named Giovanni. He seemed really upset. Madder than I've ever seen him."

"Do you have any idea who Bruno or Giovanni were?"

"None at all. I didn't want to admit I'd overheard, so I didn't ask."

"Can you remember anything else?"

Mary tapped her lip with her forefinger. "This is going to sound odd, but Trent seemed to be afraid of this Giovanni, but he also had a tone that indicated respect."

"Respect? Like perhaps a cruel father figure?"

"Maybe."

"Did you hear anything else?"

Mary shook her head. "I felt bad for listening, so I moved on down the hall."

"Old Man Johnson mentioned someone Trent referred to as Reenie. Does that ring a bell?"

"No, I'm afraid not."

"Did Trent ever mention any siblings or other family members to you?"

Mary thought about it. "I can't say that he did. I got the idea that his childhood was painful. I don't know this for certain, but I think he was brought up in a family situation grounded in neglect and possibly abuse. He was always really good with my kids, but he seemed uncomfortable around them. He usually planned to stop by when the kids were at school, but he knew I was desperate to have the plumbing fixed. He told me he planned to go out of town for a while, so it seems he spent what turned out to be the last weekend of his life finishing my plumbing upgrade before he was to leave."

"Did he say where he planned to go?"

"No, just that something had come up and he had to go away for a while. After he was done here, he said he had a job to finish up for you, but I got the feeling he planned to leave right after that. I guess he won't be taking that trip now." Mary wiped a tear from her cheek. "Who would do something like this?"

"I don't know, but I plan to find out."

By the time I left Mary's, the snow was back and I decided it might be a good idea to stop by the market to pick up some canned goods and other supplies, as Ernie had suggested when I was there on Sunday. Luckily, the soup was still on sale for a dollar a can. I threw some refrigerator biscuits into my basket as well. After stocking up on several other nonperishables, I headed toward the produce aisle, and then the dairy case. "So what do you think?" I asked Charlie. "Chocolate or vanilla?"

"More ice cream?" Ernie asked as he walked up behind us.

"More? This is the first I've bought since Christmas. I used up the last of the vanilla I had the other night with the brownies."

"Oh, I just figured the four half gallons Zak bought a while back were for you. I've never known him to buy much ice cream until a month or so ago, and I'd heard—" Ernie stopped in midsentence and actually blushed.

"The ice cream wasn't for me. He has a guest staying at his house. I suppose it could have been for the guest."

"Yes, well, I'm sure that's it. Is there anything I can help you with? I got in some fresh strawberries I haven't even put out yet. They'd go nicely with that ice cream. I'd be happy to throw in a basket."

"Strawberries sound good."

I glanced at Charlie with a look that said, *See, I told you Zak was up to no good.* Ernie was right; Zak wasn't a fan of ice cream. If he'd bought four cartons, it had to be for his guest . . . a guest, I believed this proved, who was of the female persuasion.

"It's going to be close to impossible to track down this Giovanni if you don't have his last name," Ellie pointed out later that evening as we shared a pitcher of beer with Levi at Mulligan's. Levi had ordered chicken wings and French fries, while Ellie and I shared a salad and a baked potato casserole.

"I know." I set my beer aside and reached for one of Levi's fries. "I'm beginning to think Trent was involved in some sort of Italian Mob situation."

"What?" Levi laughed. "Mary remembers a phone call during which a couple of names traditionally considered to be Italian are mentioned and suddenly Trent is part of the Mafia? Besides, Trent Everett is hardly a typically Italian name."

"Maybe," I conceded, "but the Mafia angle makes as much sense as anything. This guy moves to town and mostly keeps to himself. He doesn't make any friends, but in his spare time he runs around town like some sort of contractor Santa. Everyone loves him, but it seems that no one really knows him. He obviously has a past, but no one seems to know what that past might be. My theory is that he was on the run and as a result changed his name and moved to this tiny, out-of-the-way village where no one would find him."

"Okay, as long as we're making up stories, where exactly is this Mafia family located?" Levi asked.

"New York," I provided. "Or somewhere near there. Trent mentioned staying with his grandparents in upstate New York when he was a kid."

"I guess we could have Zak look into Mob bosses named Giovanni in New York State," Levi said. "Where is Zak, anyway?"

"Eating ice cream with someone who isn't me," I complained as I refilled my mug.

"Come again?" Ellie asked.

I explained Ernie Young's comment about the ice cream and Zak's phone call earlier, letting me know that he'd be busy all night and would catch up with me tomorrow. "It's clear to me that he's having an affair."

"I will admit that Zak has been acting a little odd lately," Ellie contributed, "but there's no way he's having an affair. He's probably working, just like he told you. Zak isn't like us. He has a *big* life. He has contracts with multinational conglomerates worth hundreds of millions of dollars. It's actually amazing that he spends as much time here in Ashton Falls as he does."

"I know. It's just that I miss him, and he keeps promising to slow down."

"And he will," Ellie predicted. "He's only been back in Ashton Falls on a full-time basis for a short time. I'm sure he had a lot of things in the works from before he decided to devote his life to making you happy."

I smiled. I had to admit he'd been pretty great at doing just that. I understood that he had a busy business life, but the ice cream and the houseguest had Jealous Zoe on full alert.

"What time do you want me to come by Ellie's on Saturday?" Levi asked Ellie.

"The earlier the better. I hope to be there by seven. I'll have coffee and homemade muffins waiting."

"Boysenberry," Levi requested.

"Boysenberry it is."

"Did you decide on the paint color?" I asked.

"Not yet. I'm going to go by to talk to your dad tomorrow. He seems to have his finger on the pulse of the paint-and-wallpaper industry."

"Yeah, he's the best," I said, in a tone that conveyed less enthusiasm than the words indicated.

"You still mad about Sunday?" Ellie asked.

"I'm not sure *mad* is the right word, but yeah, I'm still upset. There's just something about Blythe. Something I don't trust. I'm pretty sure she's trouble; I just don't know exactly what her game is quite yet."

"Have you considered," Levi asked, "that she doesn't have a game? Maybe she's exactly who she says she is."

"Look, I know you think my problem with Blythe is all wrapped up in my jealousy of any woman who might monopolize my dad's time. But I promise you that's not it. There's something not quite right about her, and I promise you I'll find out what it is."

Chapter 5

Thursday, February 6

The snow had temporarily stopped by the next morning, although the sky was heavy with clouds just waiting to dump the couple of feet of snow the National Weather Service predicted would fall by the weekend. Charlie and I took advantage of the brief reprieve to shovel the snow off the decks, then go for a quick snowshoe. I'd secretly hoped that Zak would miss me so much that he'd work things out and stop by the previous evening, but he hadn't. I don't know why I was so surprised about the number of hours Zak seemed to work. He was a successful businessman who'd made millions in the computer software industry. While Levi, Ellie, and I had spent our high-school years attending football games and going to weekend parties, Zak had built a software company in his garage, which he'd sold for tens of millions of dollars by the time he was twenty-one. For the next few years, he'd traveled the world, but he'd recently decided to start a new enterprise and had moved back to Ashton Falls. At least he lived here full-time in theory, though he tended to spend a lot of time traveling to business meetings of one type or another.

I made a fresh pot of coffee and then went into shower to dress for the busy day ahead. Zak had somehow managed to pull some strings, and the county had completed the inspection and signed off on the permits, allowing us to open on time. The only concession was that we would be unable to use the cages located in the hallway where Trent's body had been found. The bear cage was located at the end of its own wing, so most of the facility was ready and waiting for the dozens of new guests Jeremy and I were expecting to accommodate.

As the day wore on, my excitement turned to despair as the much-anticipated opening of Zoe's Zoo came and went without any animals being dropped off or a single call concerning a stray dog or nuisance wildlife was received. I'm not sure what I was expecting exactly, but I certainly wasn't anticipating that no one would even drop by.

"Maybe people figured with the murder investigation, the Zoo opening would be delayed again," Jeremy offered. "We've changed the opening day about a million times. I guess people must have lost track."

"Maybe. Still, it seems like we would have gotten a call from *someone*. Are you sure the phone lines are working?"

"Checked them seven times," Jeremy confirmed.

"I figured it might take a while to get back into our old groove, but the total absence of customers makes me feel like the community doesn't really need us," I complained.

"They need us." Jeremy put his arm around my shoulder. "We've been closed for three months. It's just going to take a while to remind people we're back."

"I guess."

"Listen, I wanted to ask if I could come in late on Wednesday of next week. Gina has a doctor's appointment and I'd really like to be there."

Gina is Jeremy's ex-girlfriend, who realized she was pregnant with Jeremy's baby last fall. She was a model at the peak of her career and planned to have the pregnancy terminated until Jeremy offered to step up, pay all of her expenses, and raise the baby on his own if she went through with the pregnancy.

"No problem," I responded. "I think it's great that you want to be involved in every step of the process. How's Gina doing, anyway?"

"Not good," Jeremy answered. "She's to the point in her pregnancy where she feels fat and bloated. She's no longer able to work and is bored to tears. I've tried to do what I can to make her comfortable and provide some level of entertainment, but everything I do seems to be wrong. I'm pretty sure she's regretting her decision to follow through with the pregnancy."

"It'll just be a few more months and then she can get on with her career, and you and Morgan can start building a life."

Jeremy's baby was due in April and he'd recently found out Gina was having a girl he planned to name Morgan Rose, after his favorite heavy-metal drummer.

"Does Gina want to be part of Morgan's life after the birth?"

My mom had only been eighteen when she realized she was pregnant with me. After my uptight and stodgy grandparents found out she was expecting, they shipped her off to an "aunt's," where I quietly, under the shroud of absolute secrecy, was delivered into the world. My grandparents wanted an anonymous adoption, but my dad fought hard and convinced them that he would raise me in isolation from the judgmental eyes of their aristocratic friends.

"She says no, but I've pretty much decided that if she ever changes her mind, Morgan and I will welcome her to participate as much or as little as she likes."

"My mom wanted nothing to do with me for the first four years of my life," I shared. "And then, out of the blue, my grandfather's representative notified my dad that she wanted to arrange a visitation."

"How'd it go?"

"Terrible. I was escorted to a huge and intimidating estate, where I cowered in the closet in spite of my mother's clumsy attempt to parent me, until someone took mercy on me and returned me to my dad."

"Sounds pretty awful. Still, Gina will always be Morgan's mother, whether she decides to act accordingly or not. I intend to make her a part of our life from the beginning. I'm planning to have photos of Gina in Morgan's room, and I'm going to make sure she knows who her mom is from an early age."

"That's probably a good idea. My dad never really talked about my mom before she appeared in my life, so the whole thing was a huge shock."

"So do you have a relationship with your mom now?"

Good question. "Not really," I answered. "She pops up now and then and we share a brief visit. She was in town last summer, but we didn't connect, although she sent me an awesome snowboard for Christmas, which is about the most thoughtful thing she's ever done. My mom has money. A lot of it. She's spent most of her life traveling the world spending it."

"Sounds awesome."

"Sounds lonely," I disagreed.

"Oh, look." Jeremy pointed toward the front window. "It looks like we have a customer."

I looked out of the window as a small boy around six or seven got out of the passenger side of a four-door sedan. He didn't appear to have an animal to drop off, so I figured he'd come by to adopt. I felt bad that we didn't have any animals *to* adopt and hoped he wouldn't be disappointed. I watched as the boy said something to the driver and then walked up the walkway Jeremy had recently shoveled. He couldn't quite manage the door on his own, so he knocked and waited for Jeremy to answer.

"This where you bring animals to get new homes?" the boy asked.

"It is," Jeremy answered. "Would you like to come in?"

Jeremy stepped aside and the boy entered.

"Do you take all kinds of animals?"

Jeremy looked at me. I nodded. How bad could it be? The kid was probably six, so I doubted he had a gorilla in the backseat of the car.

"We take most kinds of animals," Jeremy confirmed.

The boy reached into his pocket and pulled out a brown-and-white hamster. "This here is Squeaky. Mom says he has to go."

"We'd love to find a home for Squeaky," Jeremy replied. "Do you have a cage?"

"No. I got him from a friend, but my mom didn't want him, so I hid him in my sock drawer. Mom did the laundry today."

"I see." Jeremy smiled. "I think we have a cage in the back. If your mom doesn't mind waiting, you can help me look for it. That way you can be assured that Squeaky is all settled before you leave."

"What's assured?"

"Comfortable," Jeremy replied.

"I want Squeaky to be comfortable. I'll ask her. Can you hold him?"

The boy handed his sweet little pet to Jeremy. It really was too bad his mom wouldn't let him keep the low-maintenance animal. I know I have a unique way of looking at things, but as far as I'm concerned, every kid needs a pet.

"I wouldn't worry about it," Zak informed me later, after I complained to him on the phone. "I'm sure the shelter will be filled with four-legged friends in need of homes in no time at all."

"I guess." I knew Zak was right, but I was still disappointed we didn't have a better turnout.

"I'll come by the Zoo to see you in the morning, since I won't be able to see you tonight."

"You won't be seeing me tonight? You just got home. I thought we'd do something together."

"It's Thursday."

"So?"

"You have book club on Thursdays."

"I could skip." I was trying for a deep, sultry voice.

"Are you getting a cold? You sound a little raspy."

"No, I'm fine." So much for sultry.

"You know I'd love to see you tonight, but I really do have a lot of work to catch up on, and doing a computer search for your victim is going to put me even further behind. I really should stay home and work, and you should go to book club as planned."

"I could come by after," I offered.

"I'll probably work late. Let's just get together tomorrow."

"Yeah, okay," I said with a sigh.

After I hung up, I decided to check all the doors and windows before setting the alarm and closing up for the day. I was fairly certain that whoever had killed Trent had simply come in through the front door, which he'd most likely left unlocked when he arrived, but the incident had left me with a temporary feeling of vulnerability. After confirming that the windows, doggy doors, and outside exits were all secure, I headed toward the larger cages in the wildlife wing of the facility. Although this part of the Zoo was still taped off, I found I couldn't quite make myself leave without checking the exits in this hallway as well.

I flipped on lights as I worked my way down the hall. The first room was a smaller enclosure with an indoor/outdoor area that had been specifically designed with raccoons in mind, of which we usually have several at any given time. Beyond the raccoon enclosure was a medium-size cage where we kept coyotes or the occasional bobcat, and beyond that were two large enclosures designed to accommodate the bears we seemed prone to attract.

As I reached for the light switch after checking to make sure everything was locked, I noticed that one of the branches of the artificial tree we had built in the middle of the room for the cubs to climb on was bent at an odd angle. I stepped into the room for a closer look and noticed something peeking out from under the artificial turf. I bent down and pulled back the flooring to discover a brass button much like the one I'd seen on the man in Rosie's earlier in the week. The longer I studied the button, the more certain I was that it belonged to the man who I'd already decided was linked to my evil "stepwitch" in a dark and sinister way.

As I did on most Thursdays, I met with the eight members of the senior-center book club to discuss the latest in literary entertainment. Most people didn't understand why I chose to hang out with this particular set of geriatrics because the generation gap was more of a gorge, but in my opinion, the depth of experience and insights of the group members more than made up for the difference in our ages.

"Wasn't sure you'd be here." Pappy kissed my cheek as I sat down next to him.

I shrugged. "Zak had work to do and I'd read the book, so I figured why not."

"How was the opening?"

"It was a bust," I admitted. "We did manage to acquire one new guest: a hamster named Squeaky. I'm pretty sure Jeremy is going to keep him, though. The little guy is really cute, and Jeremy spent most of the day playing with him."

"Sorry to hear you didn't have a better turnout. I suppose folks might have been put off by the body that was found in your cage. Any word on who might have killed that nice young man?"

"Not officially. I found a button in the cage while I was locking up," I informed him. "I'm certain it belonged to a man I ran into at Rosie's. I took the button to Salinger, who said he'd look into it."

"You're talking about the man who thought Blythe was someone named Adriana?" Pappy asked.

"Yeah. How did you know?"

"Your dad mentioned it. He was telling me about your lunch, and it came up."

"Can you believe Dad's actually thinking of moving in with that woman?"

"I wouldn't worry too much. I get the impression he's just toying with the idea, that he's far from being committed to a course of action."

"I hope you're right. It's much too soon. Besides, I'm pretty much convinced Dad's new girlfriend is evil."

"Evil?" Pappy laughed. "Why would you say that?"

"For one thing, I'm certain she recognized the guy in the café, in spite of the fact that she flat-out lied about it."

"I don't know," Pappy countered. "These things happen. There are a surprisingly large number of people walking around who look like people we know."

"I suppose." I had to admit I'd had similar experiences, when I'd thought I recognized someone I knew but it had turned out the two individuals simply had similar features.

"What happened after the man called Blythe Adriana?" Pappy asked.

"Dad made a comment about the guy interrupting our meal, and he apologized and left."

"And Blythe?"

"She said she was ready to go. She didn't want to be late for the movie they planned to see, even though it didn't start for another two hours. She got up, and Dad followed her out of the door."

"The encounter doesn't really sound all that suspicious to me."

"What about the button I found? What if the guy from the diner is mixed up in Trent's death? Oh God." I paled. "What if Blythe is somehow mixed up in Trent's death? I have to call Dad."

"Why would Blythe kill Trent?" Pappy asked.

"I don't know, but what if the guy in the restaurant wasn't mistaken? The witch only recently moved to Ashton Falls. What if her real name is Adriana and she changed her name when she moved? What if she's really a serial killer or a foreign spy?"

"Foreign spy?" Pappy raised an eyebrow.

"Okay, she's probably not a spy, but the fact that this random guy spoke to her in the restaurant and then I found a button from his shirt at the scene of a murder can't be a coincidence. I need to warn Dad that he might be shacking up with a killer or, at the very least, a killer assistant."

"You'll do nothing of the kind," Pappy warned me. "If you start throwing around unsubstantiated allegations, you're only going to make your dad mad. He's already pretty exasperated about the fact that you don't like the woman he seems to have fallen for."

"But what if she ax murders him in his sleep?"

"You've been watching too many movies."

"Really? My contractor is shot at a facility I run and partially own and the man I saw approach Blythe just happened to lose a button at that very site on the very day I ran into him?"

"Okay, how about this," Pappy suggested. "I'll stop by your dad's house after book club. I'll tell him about the button, then let him draw his own conclusions."

I really would have preferred to talk to my dad myself, but Pappy's plan wasn't a bad one. My dad would just think I was being Jealous Zoe if I brought it up, but if Pappy approached him with the information, he might be more apt to take it into consideration.

"Okay," I finally conceded. "But be sure to mention that I found a brass button. The shirt the guy wore was so far out of style, I'm certain Dad must have noticed."

After book club, I called Zak, who informed me that he was still working and would see me in the morning. I told him about the encounter in the restaurant, and he promised to do some snooping if he had the chance. I then called Ellie, who was out with Rob and some of the other single parents. So I tried Levi, who agreed to meet me at Mulligan's for a drink.

"I'm glad you called," Levi said as I slipped into the booth next to him. "I decided to have *the talk* with Barbie tonight."

"You broke up with her?"

"I did." Levi took a swig of his beer.

"How did she take it?"

Levi frowned. "Not well. And when I say *not well*, what I mean is that she turned into a total lunatic who started crying and throwing things at me."

"Oh no." I laughed. I knew laughter was an inappropriate response, given the circumstances, but I couldn't help it.

Levi started laughing in return. "At least I broke the news to her at her apartment and not mine, so it was her stuff that was damaged."

"Sounds like that was a smart move."

"I really didn't expect her to get quite so upset." Levi shook his head. "She's such a flirt, the way she comes on to every guy she sees. I figured when I told her I wasn't ready for a serious relationship, she'd blow if off and go find some other guy to shack up with."

"Maybe she really cared about you," I suggested.

"I don't think it's that. If I had to guess, I'd be willing to bet that no guy has ever broken up with her before."

"Really? Never?"

"You've seen her."

Levi had a point. Barbie was the spitting image of every guy's fantasy. Big top, shapely bottom, tiny middle, long blond hair, blue eyes, and a killer smile.

"I get your point. Still, I think it was the right thing to do."

"Yeah, me too," Levi agreed. "So what's going on in Zoeland?"

"Why do you think something is going on?"

"Because you called me at nine o'clock on a weeknight and insisted that we go for a drink, even though I just saw you this morning and you didn't say a word about getting together."

Levi always has been pretty perceptive.

"Well, for starters, I'm pretty sure my dad is dating a murdering witch and no one but me seems overly concerned about it. Add to that the fact that I'm also sure Zak is having a steamy affair with some skank who he's hiding in his house. It really wasn't my best day. I guess I just needed a friend's shoulder to cry on."

"Zak isn't having an affair," Levi said with certainty.

"How do you know?"

"Because I know Zak. He adores the ground you walk on. Trust me: the guy is totally in love with you. I don't know what's going on to make you suspect him of an affair, but I can assure you you're dead wrong."

"And Mommystein?"

"I doubt she's a killer, but I wouldn't be a friend if I didn't at least ask why you think she is."

I explained about the man from Rosie's and the case of mistaken identity. Then I explained how Blythe got uncomfortable when he came over to the table, and how she left shortly after. And I explained about his out-of-style shirt and the brass button I'd found in the bear cage. I was certain Blythe *had* known the man in the café, and I was equally sure the man was the stranger Pack Rat had seen at the Zoo. The same stranger, I was convinced, who had killed poor, innocent Trent. If the man had killed Trent and Blythe had lied about knowing him, the only conclusion was that Blythe was somehow in on the whole thing.

"And then . . ." I was saying as my phone rang. I looked at the caller ID. It was Pappy.

"Did you talk to him?" I jumped right in as soon as I answered.

"I did."

"And?"

"It seems Salinger traced the button back to a man by the name of Anthony Martucci."

"They can use a button to identify the person who wore it?"

"Sort of. I guess once you brought the button in, Salinger rechecked the fingerprints that were found. He ran them again, and they matched Martucci's. I forwarded you a photo of the man I got from your dad."

"My dad had a photo of him?"

"Salinger showed up at his door a while ago with the photo. I scanned it and e-mailed it to you."

"Okay, hang on."

I checked my e-mail and gasped. When I got back onto the phone, I said, "That's him. That's definitely the man in Rosie's."

"Well, apparently, Blythe and your dad aren't as certain. According to the conversation I had with the pair, Blythe is insisting the man who came in was shorter, with a slighter build and lighter hair, and your dad said he couldn't really remember."

"What?" I couldn't believe what I was hearing. I half expected Blythe to continue to deny knowing the guy, but I didn't think both Dad and Blythe would deny the man in the café and the man in the photo were one and the same.

"Listen, Zoe, I know you think your dad's new friend is part of some big conspiracy, but don't you think you might be seeing a connection where one doesn't really exist? I mean, you've made it abundantly clear you aren't a fan of Blythe, and now she's campaigning to make herself an even bigger part of your dad's life than she already is. Isn't it a teensy bit possible that the guy in the photo looks like the guy in Rosie's because you want him to?"

"No, it's not a teensy bit possible I'm mistaken. I'm telling you that the guy who most likely killed Trent and the guy who talked to Blythe are one and the same, and I'm going to prove it."

I hung up the phone without saying good-bye and was immediately sorry. It wasn't Pappy's fault that Blythe was somehow hypnotizing everyone except me into seeing what she wanted them to see. The woman was evil. She'd probably cast some reality-altering spell over everyone, and seething hatred, which I happened to possess, was the only antidote.

"Wrong guy?" Levi asked.

"No, it's the right guy. Blythe has just somehow managed to convince everyone that I didn't see what I know I saw. There were other people in the restaurant. Someone else has to remember the guy."

"What about Ellie?" Levi asked.

"She was getting Stepwitch her tea. I'm pretty sure she was in the kitchen the entire time."

"Other diners?"

"There weren't a lot of people eating at the time."

Levi took my hand. "You know I love you, but isn't there a chance you're remembering what you saw just a little bit wrong? You have the tendency to go kind of crazy when anyone messes with your relationships, and Blythe has been doing a hatchet job on your relationship with your dad."

I looked Levi directly in the eye. "I'm not crazy."

"I never said you were."

"No, but you insinuated it."

"I didn't. I just think you should think things through a bit. Maybe the guy in the photo and the guy in the café are the same person. It still wouldn't mean Blythe had anything to do with killing Trent."

"It's the only thing that makes sense."

"No." Levi squeezed my hand. "It isn't. If you start accusing Blythe of being a killer without more proof, it isn't going to end well."

"So what do I do?"

Levi scooted around and put his arm around me. I laid my head on his shoulder. "We," he assured me, "will investigate. But," he qualified, "we're going to approach our investigation in a logical and unemotional manner. Okay?"

"Okay."

"No more Zoe the Crazy?"

"No more Zoe the Crazy."

Chapter 6

Friday, February 7

I woke up the next morning to sheets of snow hitting the windows overlooking the lake. It seemed Ernie Young from the general store had been right about the blizzard. I momentarily considered going back to bed—after all, the Zoo didn't actually have any animals that needed to be cared for—but then I looked out of the front window and realized that someone, probably Zak, had been by to plow out my drive. Have I mentioned what a fantastic boyfriend I have? I know I'm often jealous and petty where my relationship with the man who tends to send my emotions into overdrive is concerned, but when I looked out of the window and saw the cleared drive . . . well, suffice it to say that diamonds wouldn't have been half as appreciated.

"How about we treat ourselves to muffins from Rosie's?" I asked Charlie, who barked his assent. Warm muffins from Rosie's, coffee to go, a depressingly empty shelter . . . I could do worse.

I fed Charlie and the cats, poured coffee into a tall white mug with a large red heart, then headed toward the shower. I figured that even though we didn't have residents quite yet, it would be a good idea to keep the outside runs shoveled and the walkways cleared, just in case someone did come by.

When I arrived at the Zoo, I was greeted by the most wonderful and surprising sight. Not only were there two cats sitting on the front counter but the unmistakable sound of dogs moving about in the back of the building could be heard as well.

"Where did all the animals come from?" I asked Jeremy as I took off my coat.

"Zak picked them up from the Bryton Lake shelter." Jeremy bent down to pet Charlie. "He left a note that indicated that you were feeling depressed about the fact that we had an empty house."

"Zak went to Bryton Lake? This morning? In the middle of a blizzard? Is he nuts?"

"Actually, I'm pretty sure he went last night. When I got here this morning, I found seven dogs, three cats, two kittens, and a note saying that he'd worked out a deal with the county. I guess Commissioner Cromwell agreed to reassign the patrol they've been sending to cover Ashton Falls since the shelter closed and allow us to handle our own domestic animal-control issues."

So that was the work that had him so occupied, I realized. "I wonder why he didn't tell me what he was doing."

"He probably didn't want you to be disappointed if things didn't work out. Not only did he drop off the animals but he plowed the lot, saving me the trouble. That's one pretty great guy you've got yourself."

"Tell me about it. I should call him."

"The note says he's tied up this morning, but he'll pick you up for lunch."

"Anything else?" I asked.

"Here," Jeremy handed me the handwritten note, "read it for yourself."

The note outlined pretty much everything Jeremy had already told me. "So how's Squeaky? I noticed you didn't bring him back today."

"I think I'm going to keep him. He has a lot of personality, and he makes for a quiet and low-maintenance roommate. Last night I was watching TV and the little guy sat on my lap for over an hour. When he got tired of the movie, he climbed down the front of the sofa and took himself to bed."

"Took himself to bed?"

"I'd left the cage door open and he went right in. Of course, I'd also left a full bowl of food as well as some fresh veggies, but it was really pretty cute. I think he'll be a perfect pet with a baby in the house."

"He really is a cute little guy, and a hamster *would* be a good pet for a baby. You never know how a dog or cat will respond to an infant. Of course, Charlie loves babies."

"It looks like Charlie's a fan of babies of all kinds." Jeremy nodded to where Charlie and one of the kittens that had been dropped off were cuddled together on the floor. "I thought I'd call Hazel to see if she's interested in adopting that little guy. She mentioned wanting a kitten a while back."

"Hazel would be perfect. The kitten seems pretty calm, and he's obviously been around dogs. If she isn't interested, you might try Willa."

"I thought about her. Zak dropped off an older cat that I originally considered for her, but he's a bit of a grouch, so I put him in the back for the time being. He seems to get along okay with people, but I don't think he's been raised around other animals, and Willa has a dog. Maybe we can ask around at the senior center. He's pretty chill, so an older person who doesn't have other animals and is home to pay adequate attention to him would be just right."

"Call Janice. I bet she'd be interested. So tell me about the dogs."

"Four male, three female, all mutts. There's a golden mix that appears to be no more than a year old. The others are well into adulthood."

"Size?"

"Four under thirty pounds, two I'd guess to be sixty-five or seventy pounds, and one over a hundred and fifty."

"Over a hundred and fifty?"

"Looks to be a Saint Bernard mix. He's a real sweetie. I'd take him myself, but Squeaky and I don't really have the room. You interested in another dog?"

"No, and I wouldn't have the room for a large dog if I did. I'm sure we can find the big guy a good home with a large yard to run in. Have you called Scott?"

Scott Walden is the local vet and a shelter volunteer. We make it a policy to make certain that all animals are neutered or spayed, current on shots, and in good health before we adopt them out.

"Not yet, but I will."

"Now that we have customers, I guess we should get to work. I'll start by cleaning the pens." I know that most people don't get a thrill out of scooping dog droppings, but at that moment I couldn't have been happier if I was lounging on the deck of a cruise ship.

The storm must have chased most of the town's citizens indoors because Rosie's was uncharacteristically empty for a Friday afternoon. Zak, who looked fantastic in his bright red sweater and faded jeans, was waiting for Charlie and me at a table near the wall of windows overlooking the lake. Most of the time the view was breathtaking, but today all that could be seen was a wall of white. Originally, Zak was going to pick me up, but I needed to buy supplies for our new doggy guests, so I arranged to meet Zak at the café instead.

"It's really coming down out there," I commented.

"The National Weather Service is calling for snow through the weekend."

"Before I forget," I began, "I really want to thank you for the dogs and cats. I can't tell you how much it meant to me to arrive at the Zoo to the sound of dogs barking in the background."

"I figured it was a good idea to prime the pump, remind folks that we're open again."

"Jeremy already has half the animals adopted. If they had stayed in Bryton Lake, who knows what would have become of them?"

"I was happy to help."

I sat quietly staring out of the window, wondering exactly what was on Zak's mind. Our conversation was perfectly polite, if not somewhat mechanical, but once the pleasantries had been taken care of, we seemed to have nothing to talk about. A stranger observing our exchange would think us casual acquaintances at best.

"I was thinking it might be nice to have dinner at your place tonight," I suggested. "We could light some candles, open a bottle of champagne, soak in the hot tub, and watch it snow."

One of the coolest things about the house Zak had bought was that it had an indoor/outdoor pool and spa with a roof that retracted as the weather dictated. The room was made of glass walls, which brought the outdoors inside during the colder winter months. An indoor/outdoor fireplace and natural stone floor made for a romantic setting year round.

"I was thinking we could go out tonight," Zak countered.

"In a blizzard?"

"I've been craving a thick, juicy steak and some of those stuffed mushrooms from the Wharf."

The Wharf is an upscale restaurant that serves seafood and steaks that are flown in fresh every day. While the food there is fabulous, my idea sounded a bit more romantic.

"We can make steaks at your place," I suggested.

"Seems like a lot of work. Besides, I've been dying to try the burgundy sauce everyone's been raving about. If the sauce is as good as I've heard, I thought I'd take some home to see if Ellie can figure out the recipe. How about I pick you up at seven?"

"Yeah, okay," I agreed with more enthusiasm than I felt.

It wasn't like Zak to choose going out over staying in. I know I'm probably just being Zoe, but I couldn't help but feel that he was intentionally trying to divert my attention from romance to recipes.

"Hey, guys," Ellie greeted us. "What can I get you?"

"I'll have a club sandwich," I said.

"Make that two," Zak agreed.

"Mom made clam chowder, if you want a cup to go with your sandwiches."

"Sounds good," I replied. Rosie made the best clam chowder.

"I'll take a cup of coffee as well," Zak added.

"Zoe?" Ellie asked.

"Water is fine."

"By the way," Zak continued after Ellie had returned to the kitchen, "I wanted to fill you in on the information I managed to dig up on Anthony Martucci. I know you think Blythe is involved with him in some way, but I couldn't find a connection between the two of them."

"What about the fact that he seemed to recognize her?" I asked. "I know this is going to sound crazy, but I can pretty much guarantee you that the man in the restaurant and the man who we suspect killed Trent are the same person. I think Blythe has hypnotized my dad into thinking he didn't see what he saw."

"You're right," Zak responded.

"I am?"

"It does sound crazy." Zak reached across the table and took my hand. "You know I care about you and I'll always be on your side, but in this instance, I think your feelings toward Blythe, while justified," he assured me, "might be coloring your judgment."

"My judgment is fine." I pulled my hand away just as Ellie arrived with our soup.

"The sandwiches are on their way," she told us as she gave me a look that questioned my obvious annoyance with Zak.

"Okay, assume that you're right," Zak continued after Ellie left to greet two men who'd just walked in. "Assume that the man whose button you found and the man you saw here are the same. What could be the possible connection between Blythe and this man, who simply appears to have been passing through town?"

I stared out of the window at the snow blowing down from the summit as I tried to wrap my head around everything Zak was sharing with me. What he was saying made sense, but I was certain Blythe knew the killer. I know it seems like I believe the woman guilty of wrongdoing because I *want* her to be guilty, but my instinct was telling me that I was right and everyone else was wrong. I thought about what I *really* knew about the woman who was out to ruin my life by seducing my poor, helpless father. I remembered that when my dad introduced me to her over Christmas, he'd mentioned that she'd just moved to the area after retiring from teaching. I don't think he mentioned where exactly it was that she'd taught, but since she'd mentioned a hairdresser in Bryton Lake, I assumed she was from there. But what if she wasn't? I couldn't help but wonder where Anthony Martucci was from, or an even better question, where he was now.

"Here are your sandwiches." Ellie was back. "Anything else?"

"Remember when I was in the other day with my dad?" I asked.

"Yeah, sure."

"Blythe came in and joined us. She ordered tea, and shortly after that a man came over and spoke to us. I know you were in the kitchen, but did you happen to see him?"

"Sorry." Ellie shook her head.

"I'm certain the guy who came in that day is the same guy the sheriff suspects of killing Trent, but I'm having a hard time convincing anyone else of it." I held up my phone so Ellie could see the photo Pappy had forwarded to me. "Does he look familiar at all?"

Ellie shook her head. "Connie was working the cash register that day," she pointed out. "Maybe she remembers something. I'm pretty sure Gage Wheeler was still here as well. He was sitting at the counter."

"Is Connie working today?" I asked.

"No. I'll call her at home to see if she saw anything," Ellie offered.

"I've got some errands to run, so I can talk to Gage," Zak said as the familiar *ding* associated with his cell phone's text chimed from his pocket. Zak pulled out his phone, looked at it, and frowned. "I have a million things to do before our date tonight. I really should get going. Go ahead and finish your sandwich."

"You're leaving?"

Zak paused. "I'm sorry. That was rude. I really do need to go. Tonight?"

"Listen, you obviously have a lot going on, so I'll stop by to talk to Gage after I finish here."

"Thanks." Zak leaned down and kissed me. "I'll pick you up at seven."

"That was abrupt," Ellie said as she slid into the booth across from me after Zak left. "What was that all about?"

"I think Zak is going to break up with me."

"What? Why would you think that?"

"It's the only thing that makes sense. I suggested a romantic evening of champagne and candlelight at his house, but he countered with dinner out at the Wharf. Then he got a text and left in the middle of lunch. And to top it off, he doesn't believe that Blythe is in cahoots with Anthony Martucci."

"Sweetie, no one but you believes that Blythe and Anthony Martucci are connected. I have to admit, though, that the rest seems odd. He does have that big project going on. Maybe he's just distracted."

"Maybe."

"I talked to Jeremy earlier. He told me about the cats and dogs. That doesn't seem like something a guy who was planning to break up with a girl would bother with."

"Yeah, I guess. It just seems like *something* is going on. Maybe I just need to put it out of my mind. How was your date with Rob last night?"

"Confusing."

"Confusing how?"

"I guess his babysitter canceled, so he asked Rick to stay with Hannah."

I grimaced. I think I could see where this conversation was going. Rick was Ellie's ex. She hadn't started dating his brother Rob until after they'd broke up, and I'd warned her at the time she started seeing Rob that there could be a conflict.

"I'd agreed to meet Rob at his house and Rick was there when I showed up. Rob was still in the shower, so Rick and I chatted. He said he missed me and was sorry we broke up. He wanted to know if we could try again."

"What did you say?"

"I said that given the fact that Rob and I had been dating, it would be awkward at best. When I first started going out with Rob, I talked to Rick about it, and he said he was perfectly fine with the situation, but now I'm not so sure he is."

"So what are you going to do?"

"Honestly, I have no idea. I really enjoy going out with Rob, but I also enjoy my friendship with Rick, although I'm pretty sure our romantic relationship had run its course by the time we broke up. If I choose one brother over the other, it's only going to lead to trouble. I suppose it would be best not to date either of them, but I really like Rob, and I feel like there could be something more in our future if we give our relationship a chance."

"Maybe you should have a heart-to-heart with Rick," I suggested. "Explain your feelings for Rob and see what he says."

"Yeah, maybe."

"A word of warning, however," I cautioned. "Rick is a fun sort of guy who doesn't appear to be ready for anything serious, while Rob is older and has a child. Based on the few casual conversations I've had with him, I think there's a very good possibility that Rob is ready to find someone to settle down with. The question is, are *you* ready for that sort of relationship?"

"Rob and I are really just friends," Ellie countered. "I doubt he's thinking about wedding bells right now."

"Maybe, but Rob has a child in need of a mother. I wouldn't be at all surprised if he didn't choose the women he dates based on their *potential* to at least fulfill that role. I could be wrong, but it wouldn't be bad to keep that in mind."

"Yeah, okay, I will."

"I need to get going." I slid out of the booth. "I want to catch Gage Wheeler before he goes home for the day."

"It's early," Ellie pointed out.

"Yeah, but Gage has a tendency to go in early and then leave shortly after lunch. I'll call you later."

Gage Wheeler owned the local lumberyard and was an active volunteer in the community. Although I wouldn't say we were close, I'd known him for years. He had a reputation for being gruff and outspoken, but he cared about his neighbors and could be counted on to roll up his sleeves and pitch in if there was a task to be accomplished. The lumberyard was located on the east edge of town and could only be accessed by a graded road. Luckily, someone had come by with a plow, so the property was accessible by a four-wheel drive vehicle.

Charlie looked out of the passenger-side window and barked as we were greeted by two large dogs as we pulled up in front of the trailer Gage used as an office. The trees surrounding the property were blanketed with snow, as were the large piles of logs waiting for processing. I knew that the large barnlike structure at the back of the property housed the lumber that had been cut and processed and was now available to be purchased by local contractors.

While the lumberyard was a busy place in the spring and summer, Gage and a couple of assistants held down the fort during the heart of the winter, when new construction was at a standstill and remodels were few and far between. I parked near the entrance to the trailer and told Charlie to wait while I climbed out of my giant truck and carefully made my way along the icy path to the front door. I knocked and waited for Gage to invite me in.

"Zoe Donovan. What are you doing all the way out here on this snowy day?"

The interior of the trailer was drab and gray, with metal desks and tall black file cabinets. There was a computer on the desk Gage was sitting behind that was probably older than I was. To the right of the desk was a locked cabinet holding several guns on display. I knew Gage was a hunter who often went into the forest for weeks at a time.

"I'm trying to round up all the keys we gave out during the remodel and wasn't sure if I'd gotten yours back or not."

"Actually, I do still have it." Gage opened the top drawer of his desk, found it, and handed it to me. "I was waiting to bring it back until I found out if you were going to need more wood for the enclosure in the bear cage. It looked like you might be short."

"I wasn't aware you'd been by to see the work we'd done."

"Stopped in the other day, when I was in the area."

"Jeremy didn't mention it."

"He wasn't there. It was after hours, so I let myself in. The offices look really nice with all the new paneling."

"Yeah, they are nice. Listen, I wanted to ask you about a man who stopped into Rosie's the other day while I was having lunch with my dad. He came in from the street, spoke briefly to Blythe, and then left. You were eating at the counter. I was hoping you'd seen him."

Gage appeared to be thinking about it.

"I'm trying to determine if the man who came in was this man." I showed him the photograph of Anthony Martucci.

Gage shook his head. "I had my back turned toward the main dining area. I remember you and your dad having lunch. I remember seeing Blythe come in. But I'm afraid I don't remember this man, although I've seen him before."

"Can you tell me where and when?"

"He was talking to Kevin Michaels in the parking lot of the grocery store. To be honest, it looked more like they were arguing."

"When was that?"

"It must have been Saturday. I was in town doing my errands."

"And you don't know what they were arguing about?"

"No, I didn't really stop to listen."

"Okay, thanks."

Gage hadn't provided the proof that I needed to convince the masses that the man I'd seen in the café was the same man who'd killed Trent, but he had given me a clear direction and a solid lead. Maybe I was getting somewhere.

I decided it might be worth my while to talk to Kevin. Not only was he one of the few people in town who knew Trent but he'd also been seen arguing with Martucci. If there was a connection between the man and Trent, Kevin might be the one to provide it.

Ashton Falls is a small town with limited opportunities when it comes to new construction, so Kevin Michaels, a general contractor who has lived and worked here for the past ten years, specializes in remodels. While he doesn't maintain a regular workforce due to the seasonality of the construction trade, he hires subcontractors and temporary help from time to time. As far as I knew, Trent had worked for Kevin ever since moving to the area the previous spring.

Trent seemed to be a good worker as well as an all-around nice guy. Of course, people who tend to keep to themselves are sometimes the very ones who have something to hide. I knew Kevin had been working on an attic conversion the previous day, so I headed toward the Mendoza house, which is located at the edge of town. As I pulled up in front of the house, I saw that Kevin's red truck was indeed in the drive. The house he was renovating was a two-story structure built on a large, open meadow overlooking the summit. While the lake views from the boathouse are breathtaking, the one from the back of this house was spectacular as well. After instructing Charlie to wait, I got out of my vehicle and made my way to the front of the house.

"Kevin inside?" I asked one of the temporary workmen Kevin had hired for the job as I slipped out of my boots, leaving them on the tile entry before stepping onto the light beige carpet.

"Yeah, he's upstairs."

"Thanks," I responded as I made my way toward the attic in my stocking feet. I could hear hammers and saws working away and realized that Kevin might not want to take a break to speak to me.

"Hey, Zoe. What brings you out here?" Kevin asked as I entered the room.

"I wanted to ask you about Trent."

"I guess I should have figured as much. How about we take this conversation downstairs, where it's not so hectic?"

"That's probably a good idea."

By the look of things, the attic wasn't the only space getting a facelift. The house was already beautiful; once Kevin and his guys were done with it, it was going to be spectacular. It appeared as though everything from flooring to light fixtures and cabinets had been stripped out to make room for the new.

"So what can I do for you?" Kevin asked as we took seats at the counter in the empty kitchen.

"Are the homeowners gone?" I looked around.

"They're vacationing in the Bahamas while the remodel is underway."

"That," I decided as I looked out of the window at the falling snow, "sounds wonderful."

"Yeah, it must be nice," Kevin agreed.

"Like I said, I wanted to ask you about Trent." I decided to get right to the subject at hand. "I know Salinger is conducting an official investigation, but I decided to do some snooping around on my own."

"Seems to me that you've been smack dab in the middle of all the murder investigations around here of late."

"Yeah, well, I guess circumstances keep pulling me in."

"Don't figure there's any harm in telling you what I know. Seems you're developing quite an impressive track record."

"Believe me when I tell you that spending all my free time investigating murders is nowhere in my overall plan. Still, Trent did die on the property I manage, and he seemed like a really nice guy. I just want to be certain that his killer is brought to justice."

"Yeah, I'd like to see that too."

"Can you tell me how Trent came to work for you?"

"He came to me last May as part of the Fresh Start program the state is sponsoring to help men and women who have spent time in prison get a new lease on life once they're released."

"So Trent was in prison," I confirmed.

"Spent the past seven years incarcerated for various Mob-related activities," Kevin elaborated. "While he was in prison, they trained him to perform various tasks in the construction industry. After he was released, I was contacted about hiring him. I agreed, and it ended up working out really well. He was actually one of my best temps. I'm going to miss him."

I watched Kevin's face as he spoke. His tone of voice seemed casual and controlled, but the twitch in his eye and the reddish tone of his skin indicated that he was more affected than he was letting on. It made sense that Kevin would be upset about Trent's death. He *had* worked closely with him for almost a year.

"Where did he live prior to his stint in prison?"

"I have no idea," Kevin admitted. "The program places their graduates in locations far from their old neighborhoods and associations. Trent made several comments, however, that led me to believe he was originally from the East Coast."

"Did he seem to have any contact with his old crowd?"

"Not as far as I know. The man kept to himself."

"So you can't think of anyone he might have hung out with socially?"

"Not a single person."

"Do you know where Trent was incarcerated?"

"No, I don't. Just so you know," Kevin informed me, "Sheriff Salinger asked me all these same questions. I'm guessing he has access to information I don't. Maybe you should ask him what he found out about Trent's past."

"Oh, yeah, that'll go over well. Can you think of anything else at all?"

"Not really. He was a hard worker and seemed to be a good guy. It's a real shame something like this happened after he'd gone to so much effort to start over again."

"Did Trent ever mention a family? Perhaps a sister?"

Kevin frowned. He tried to control his expression, but I was certain he'd momentarily conveyed something I can only describe as concern. "No, he never mentioned family. In fact, I'm pretty sure he mentioned being an only child."

I took out my phone and showed Kevin the photo of Martucci. "Do you know this man?"

I noticed the tightening of Kevin's jaw as his level of stress seemed to increase. "I don't really know him, but I did speak to him the other day. Is he mixed up in Trent's murder?"

"Maybe. Can you tell me what you talked about?"

"He asked if I knew a guy by the name of Joey Marino. I told him that I didn't. He described the man he was looking for and I suspected he might be describing Trent, but I didn't say as much. I knew Trent had been trying to leave his old life behind, and the guy I spoke to had that look about him."

"Look?"

"Like he was in the Mob or something. He had on the strangest clothes, which I suspect he believed would help him to blend in but instead made him stand out."

"Black shirt with brass buttons?" I guessed.

"Exactly."

"So what did you say to him?"

"I told him I had no idea who this Joey was, and he insisted that it appeared I was lying. I didn't take kindly to the accusation and told him so. He was obviously angry, but he left without things becoming physical."

"Have you seen him since?"

"No. He did tell me that he was staying at the River Ranch Motor Inn. In case I remembered anything that might help him."

"Thanks for your help." I turned to leave. "One last thing: did Trent ever mention someone named Reenie?"

"No. Never. Now I really need to get back to work."

"Okay. Thanks again."

I know this is going to sound nuts, but at that moment, I really thought the best idea was for me to pay our suspected killer a little visit.

The drive to the outskirts of town was beautiful as the branches of the evergreen trees that lined the road drooped under the weight of freshly fallen snow. It looked like the county plow had made a single run, leaving a thick sheet of ice on the narrow road. Luckily, not only is my truck a four-wheel drive, it's a four-wheel monster that was normally able to plow its way through even the deepest drifts of snow.

The River Ranch Motor Inn, a run-down motel most often frequented by hunters, is located at the end of an isolated rutted dirt road that, today, was covered with snow. Most of the time, the owner keeps the drive plowed, but from time to time the path becomes impassable. Normally, the River Ranch closes for the winter months, but I suspected that with the influx of skiers we'd had since the opening of the new resort on the west shore of the lake, the motivation to keep the facility open had increased.

I pulled under the overhang that shielded the front door from the worst of the weather. Luckily, the lot had been plowed down to the thick red mud of the dirt surface. I wasn't thrilled about picking my way through it, and told Charlie to stay as I slid out of the truck and made my way carefully to the office. The lobby was deserted, but the sound of a television in the background led me to believe someone was around.

"Hello," I shouted loud enough to be heard in the back room. I waited as an elderly man let out a curse before muting the action thriller he'd been watching.

"Can I help you?"

"I'm looking for a friend who's staying here. His name is Anthony Martucci."

The man looked me up and down, as if deciding whether or not to give me the information I'd requested. "He expecting you?"

"No, but I'm a friend. I heard he was in town and wanted to surprise him."

The man seemed to consider my request, then shrugged. "Room twelve. Last door on the left side of the building. He might not take kindly to your visit, though. He paid for a week in advance and asked not to be disturbed. He even requested not to have maid service. To be honest, I don't think he's left his room in days."

"Thank you for the heads-up. I guess it wouldn't hurt to knock on the door. After a week, he might be ready for some company." I smiled and retreated into the cold. I decided to pull my truck around to the empty parking spot in front of room 10. The only other car in the lot was a blue sedan parked in front of Martucci's room. If I had to guess, that car most likely belonged to Martucci, indicating that he was indeed in residence. I got out of my truck, being careful to step over the worst of the muddy puddles, and then wiped my feet on the cement walkway as I knocked on the door. As I stood there waiting, it suddenly occurred to me that I had no idea what I was going to say if the man answered. Have I mentioned that I tend to be a bit impulsive, and, more often than not, that tendency seems to get me in trouble?

I waited for over a minute and had pretty much decided to leave when I realized that the sound of the movie the desk clerk had been watching could clearly be heard from where I stood. It was possible the sound was coming from the room next door, but since the place seemed to be deserted, I knocked once again. After several seconds, I tried the doorknob, which turned easily. Against my own better judgment, I opened the door and stepped inside.

Anthony Martucci was lying on the floor in a pool of blood. Based on the level of decomposition, I was willing to bet he'd been dead for quite some time.

Chapter 7

Saturday, February 8

The blizzard had died down to a flurry the next morning, so Charlie and I went out for a snowshoe. I love the forest after a storm. The branches of the evergreens surrounding the boathouse hung low with the weight of their burden, the fresh snow turning the landscape into a clean, crisp white. I live on an isolated cove, so the snow on the beach was unmarred by tracks as Charlie and I struggled to plow through the deep drifts.

As hard as I tried, I couldn't get the image of Martucci's lifeless eyes out of my head. I'd seen dead bodies before; more than would seem normal, I had to confess. But Martucci was the only murder victim I'd come across who was staring back with sunken eyes. It appeared that he'd been hit over the head with something heavy enough to crush the back of his skull. Then he'd fallen forward, after which someone—I assume the killer—had turned him over onto his back.

According to Salinger, the man had been dead for several days. He was waiting for an official autopsy, but the sheriff was willing to speculate that if Martucci had been involved in Trent's murder, *he* must have been killed later the same night. I realized that it was going to be hard to prove that a dead man killed Trent, and probably even harder to figure out who killed the killer. My money was still on Blythe being involved in some way, but according to pretty much everyone I talked to, I was alone in my suspicion.

I hadn't planned to travel far due to the difficulty of navigating the fresh powder, but before I even realized where I was headed, I found myself standing at the back of Zak's mansion. Things between us had continued to be strange. Dinner the previous evening had been nice. The food was good, the atmosphere romantic, yet somehow I couldn't help but wish we'd been eating sandwiches at Zak's kitchen counter. I could tell he was trying to be an attentive companion, sharing funny stories over dinner, which was followed by slow dancing to seductive music. By anyone's standards, the night had been magical. So why, I had to ask myself, had Zak declined my invitation to stay the night? I'd suffered a sleepless night, with images of dead men in my dreams, and I really needed someone with whom I could share my thoughts and feelings.

I was about to turn around to head back home when I saw a light come on in the kitchen. Based on the height of the figure walking in front of the drawn blinds, the person rummaging for breakfast wasn't Zak. I knew before I even started toward the back deck that I was going to regret my rash behavior, but as I've already pointed out, no one has ever accused me of being anything less than impulsive.

I peeked in through a kitchen window that didn't have a blind pulled all the way down. I was greeted by the backside of a small woman dressed in black tights with her head buried deep in the refrigerator.

"Zak," she called, "are those cartons of yogurt you bought gone?"

I frowned at the voice. She sounded an awful lot like . . . "Mom?" I gasped as the woman emerged from the depths of the refrigerator. She turned around and faced the window I was peering through. I'm not sure exactly what happened after that, but the next thing I knew, I was lying on Zak's sofa and a very concerned Charlie was licking my face.

"Zoe, are you okay?" Zak asked as he stroked my hair.

"What happened?" I asked as I struggled to sit up.

"You passed out. It's a good thing Charlie started barking or we might not have known you were out on the deck. You could have frozen to death."

We? And then I remembered. "My mother is here," I accused.

"I know. I wanted to tell you."

"And she's *pregnant*! How could you?" I put my hand to my head as my dizziness returned.

"I wanted to tell you." Zak held me in his arms. "I almost did several times, but your mom didn't want you to know she was here until she had time to figure everything out. She made me promise not to tell."

"Well, I should guess so." I pulled away from Zak. "How could you hide my mother from me?"

"I'm sorry, but it's a complicated situation."

"Complicated?" I yelled. "You think this is complicated?"

"Look, I know you're upset that I didn't tell you your mom was here, but now that you know, we can sit down and talk things out."

"You've been sleeping with my *mother* and you want to *talk* about it?"

"What?" Zak looked shocked. "I'm not sleeping with your mother. God, Zoe. How could you even suggest such a thing?"

"She's staying in your house. You've been lying about it. *And* she's pregnant," I pointed out.

"The baby isn't mine," Zak informed me. "I can't believe you'd think it was."

He looked hurt. Maybe I'd been just a tiny bit rash in my assumptions.

"Then whose is it?"

Zak hesitated. "I think that's a question you should ask your mom. She went upstairs to change. She got soaking wet when she rushed out to help you after you passed out. I didn't want her to get chilled."

I looked at Zak. He seemed both hurt and sincere. Suddenly, I felt like an idiot. I'm not sure if it was the stress or some sort of delayed relief, but I started to cry. Zak picked me up and carried me upstairs. He helped me to peel off my wet clothes, wrapped me in a robe several sizes too big for me, then walked with me back downstairs, where my mother was waiting.

I had no idea what to say to a woman about whom I'd harbored so many conflicting emotions, so I didn't say anything as I walked across the room and wrapped my arms around her. We both cried, sharing an embrace without words until, eventually, I pulled back and looked her in the face.

"You're pregnant," I stated the obvious.

"Yeah." She looked uncertain.

I smiled. "I'm going to be a big sister."

Mom smiled back. "I guess you are."

We hugged again as Zak set coffee and fresh muffins on the table.

"Why did you keep this a secret?" I asked. "I would have understood. These things happen, and you were engaged." Prior to her visit last summer, my mom had been planning to marry the prince of some small country I'd never heard of.

"The baby doesn't belong to the prince," my mom informed me.

"Not the snowboard developer?" I groaned. Mom had only known him a short time.

"No, not him either."

"Then who?"

My mom blushed, and suddenly I knew.

"Dad," I realized.

My mom looked down at her hands.

"But how?" I asked. "I don't mean *how*. I know *that*." Now I was blushing. "What I mean is why? No, not why." I looked at Zak. "Help me out here."

"Let's sit down," Zak suggested.

He led Mom and me over to one of the three sofas arranged around the two-story fireplace. After we settled in, I waited for Mom to speak. She seemed to be working up her courage to tell her story, which I was certain was going to be an emotional roller coaster for both of us.

"After becoming engaged to Rafael," Mom began—I later learned that was the name of her prince—"I started thinking about my life. I was only eighteen when I became pregnant with you, and I let my parents convince me that having a child would ruin my life. When your dad wanted to adopt you, it seemed easy to let him do it. I always loved you," Mom assured me. "From the first moment I held you in my arms and looked into your eyes, I knew we'd always be bonded on some level, but I also knew I could never be the mother you deserved. So I gave you to your father and went away."

I had so many questions, but I decided it was best to let Mom tell the story in her own way.

"I know it may not appear that way," she continued, "but I've always loved your father. I've traveled the world and had many exotic love affairs, but every night when I'd wish upon a star, it was his face I'd see in my mind."

"Why didn't you come back?" I asked.

"I don't know. I guess I was scared. I didn't want to risk destroying the fantasy I'd created by requiring it to stand up to the test of reality, so I spent my years dreaming about a love I was too scared to subject to possible rejection. After I got engaged to Rafael, I decided I couldn't go through with the wedding until I knew for certain. So I came back to Ashton Falls and knocked on your dad's door."

"He must have been shocked." I smiled.

"Shocked is putting it mildly."

"What did he say?"

"Nothing. I walked into his arms, he kissed me, and your baby sister was conceived. Neither of us said a single word until afterward."

"And then?"

"Then I guess reality checked in. Your dad told me that while my showing up on his doorstep was the subject of every fantasy he'd ever had, he didn't know if he could put himself out there again. We talked and decided to see each other but take it slow. I rented a little house at the beach and we began dating. We agreed not to tell you that I was back until we were certain it was going to work out."

"You left," I accused.

"I found out I was pregnant and panicked. I'm not making any excuses. I handled the whole thing badly. I went to my parents' place in Switzerland and tried to figure out what I was going to do."

"And?"

"After much soul-searching, I decided to keep the baby. I decided I wanted to be part of this daughter's life in a way I never had been part of yours. I also realized that your father had a right to know his daughter as well, so I decided to come back and talk things out with him."

"So why are you here?" I asked. "At Zak's house? Why aren't you with Dad? I assume he doesn't know?"

"When I got here, I found out he was involved with another woman," Mom explained. "I didn't know what to do, so I called Zak, and he agreed to let me stay here until I figured things out."

"Why Zak? I wasn't aware you even knew each other."

"We're business partners. We actually talk quite often."

"Business partners?" I frowned. Then, "The Zoo," I realized. "You're the silent partner in the Zoo. Why didn't you tell me?"

"I don't know." Mom smiled sadly. "When I heard what Zak planned to do, I knew I wanted to be part of it. Being a part owner in the Zoo made me feel close to you in a strange sort of way. I didn't want to complicate things by making my involvement public, so Zak and I agreed on a silent partnership. In the course of working through the legalities, we've become friends."

I put my head in my hands and tried to process everything. I found that I was thrilled to have my mom back in my life, and excited to know that I was going to finally have the sibling I'd always longed for. At the same time, I had an overwhelming feeling of dread in the pit of my stomach that I couldn't quite identify.

"We have to tell Dad," I insisted.

"I don't want to mess up his relationship with Blythe. He's a good man. He deserves his heart's desire."

"Blythe is evil," I insisted. "Maybe if Dad knows about you and the baby, he'll break up with that witch and I won't have to worry about her ax-murdering him in his sleep."

"What?" Mom looked at Zak.

"I'm afraid the situation isn't as clear-cut as Zoe makes it sound," Zak explained. "There's been a murder in town, and Zoe is convinced Blythe is mixed up in it in some way, but as far as I can tell, the evidence is far from conclusive."

"The woman does have a strange aura," Mom contributed.

"Ha!" I pointed at Zak, thrilled that *someone* other than me saw the woman for what she really was. "Wait," I added. "How do you know about her aura? Have you seen her?"

"From a distance," Mom admitted.

Zak didn't actually say anything, but I could tell by the look on his face that he realized he was in for an uphill battle now that both Mom and I distrusted the witch.

"What if Zoe is right?" Mom asked.

"It seems unlikely at this point," Zak answered.

"But what if she's right? If we look into it and she's wrong, no harm. If we assume she's wrong and she's not, Hank could be in real trouble."

"Good point," Zak admitted. "Okay, let's get on the computer and see what we can find out."

After we decided to dive into the murder case with both guns loaded, Zak took me home so I could change into dry clothes. I got in touch with Jeremy, who was more than happy to take care of the chores at the Zoo on his own, then called Ellie to cancel the lunch we'd planned. It felt strange not to include Levi and Ellie in our discussion, but Mom wasn't quite ready to come out, so I agreed to keep her secret for the time being.

The idea of being a big sister both thrilled and terrified me. I'd longed for a sibling when I was a child, but there'd also always been a part of me that enjoyed being daddy's little girl. I knew my father loved me and would always love me, but I also realized that with the return of my mother and the birth of my sister, the dynamic we'd always known would inevitably change.

Still, to have my mom in my life, and to have a sister . . . Change had always been difficult for me, but in this case, I had to assume that the change would be for the better. Besides, I *really* was too old to play the part of the deserted elder child, in spite of any doubts that might linger.

After I changed, Zak and I returned to his house and settled in at the computer.

"Okay, here's what we know," Zak began. "A local contractor by the name of Trent Everett was shot in the bear cage at Zoe's Zoo. Zoe found a button that belonged to a man by the name of Anthony Martucci, who we believe killed Trent. Zoe quite unwisely went to speak to Mr. Martucci and found him dead in his motel room."

"You went to his motel alone?" Mom looked shocked.

"I guess I didn't think things through."

"You could have been killed."

"I thought of that *after* I found the body."

"Anyway," Zak continued, "Zoe believes she saw Martucci come into Rosie's while she was having lunch with Hank and Blythe. Blythe has stated that the man who came in and referred to her as Adriana wasn't the same guy, and Hank says he isn't sure."

"I guess the man in the photo and the one who spoke to Blythe *could* be different people," Mom said.

"Maybe, but I'm pretty sure they're not," I insisted. "I hoped the cashier at Rosie's would recognize the guy, but when I called to cancel lunch with Ellie she said she'd talked to Connie, who couldn't be certain if the man in the photo was the man who came in that day. She confirmed that he had similar features, but she wouldn't swear to them being the same."

"So what now?" Mom asked.

"We need to find out everything we can about Blythe and look for a connection, if one exists," Zak answered.

"Maybe do a Google search?" Mom suggested. "At the very least, we should be able to find surface information such as last known address and professional affiliations."

"Okay, give me a minute." Zak started typing.

"So you're having a girl?" I asked Mom while Zak worked.

"She's due in April." Mom ran a hand over her stomach. "Do you want to feel her kick?"

I placed my hand on Mom's stomach. The entire situation was so surreal that I had to wonder if I was dreaming. I jumped when she kicked me.

"Did you feel her?" Mom asked.

"I did. I'm going to have a sister." I smiled. "Do you have a name picked out?"

"I have a few I'm considering. Any suggestions?"

I'd never really thought about what I'd name a baby, but coming up with the perfect name intrigued me. I liked the idea of a name with meaning rather than just something random based on the popular soft drink of the moment. "Can I think about it?"

"Absolutely. I want you to be a big part of this baby's life. I have a lot to learn about being a mom, and I'm really going to need your help."

"Like I know anything about being a mom." I laughed.

"Oh, but you do. I've seen you with the animals. The way you care for and nurture them. You're a mom every day. It's just that your kids are a bit on the furry side."

I laughed again. I can't tell you how wonderful it felt that my mom not only wanted me in her life but apparently *needed* me. My mind immediately jumped to the million and one things I had to do and learn before my very special little sister was born.

"That's odd," Zak said.

"What's odd?" I asked.

"There are no fingerprints on record for a Blythe Ravenwood. If she was a teacher, she would have been fingerprinted."

"So maybe she really isn't a retired teacher," I speculated.

"Or maybe she taught under a different name," Mom offered.

"Maybe." Zak continued to type. "It looks like Blythe Spalding married Tim Ravenwood in November 2010," Zak informed us.

"She's married?" I gasped.

"No," Zak answered. "Tim passed away in February 2011. The couple lived in Denver, where Tim owned a chain of dry cleaners. Tim apparently died of a heart attack, although he was only forty-four."

I hated to admit it, but at that moment I actually felt bad for Blythe.

"Anything else?" I asked as my phone began to ring. "Hey, Dad. What's up?" I answered before Zak could respond to my inquiry.

Mom's face furrowed in concern as I listened to my dad requesting a get-together in an hour. I suppose she was afraid I'd blurt out the identity of Zak's special guest, but she should have known me well enough to be sure I'd never do such a thing. The saddest thing was, the woman who gave me birth knew my boyfriend a lot better than she did her own daughter.

"An hour is fine," I answered. "See you then."

Mom let out the breath she'd been holding as I hung up. "Don't worry," I assured her. "I won't say anything about, well, anything."

"Thanks. I'm going to tell him. When the time is right."

"Do you think that's ever really going to happen?" I asked. "Do you think the time to share this particular piece of news will ever really be right?"

"Probably not," she admitted.

"Dad wants me to come over so he can talk to me about something."

"You go and do that, and I'll keep digging," Zak said.

During the entire trip to my dad's house, I kept playing over again and again in my mind the horror of his anticipated announcement that he was moving in with the woman I was certain was a cold-blooded killer. I tried to imagine a reaction he would listen to, but no matter how many scenarios I ran through, I came up blank. I suppose there was the very slight possibility that the *talk* he wanted to have had nothing to do with the evil stepwitch, but my luck hadn't been all that great as of late, so the chances of a reprieve were slight.

"Dad," I called as I let myself in through the front door. I'd decided to leave Charlie at home in case things got ugly.

"In the den," he called back.

I walked down the hallway with all the dread of a condemned prisoner making his journey to the death chamber. I loved my dad and didn't want to say or do anything that would cause him to think less of me, but I knew in my heart that I'd never be able to accept Momzilla into my life. I sighed in relief when I walked into the room to see Dad alone with his dogs, Tucker and Kiva.

"Thanks for coming so quickly. I hope I didn't interrupt anything."

"No. Zak and I were just messing around on the computer." I sat down on the chair opposite my dad. "What's up?"

"Blythe is having her home fumigated and wants to stay with me for a few days. I hoped that you could take Tucker and Kiva while she's here. I'm afraid she's not a big fan of the dogs."

That's it? He wants me to babysit his dogs? Who has their house fumigated in the middle of winter? Still, I was happy that the subject of our conversation wasn't a more permanent arrangement between my dad and Blythe, so I let it go. I wanted to ask what he was going to do with the dogs he loved so much if he decided to make his living arrangement with Hagula permanent but decided not to push my luck.

"I'd be happy to," I said. "You know they're always welcome at my house."

"I really appreciate it. Blythe has assured me that we're talking two or three days at the most."

"No problem."

"Is there anything else on your mind?" I asked. Dad seemed nervous and fidgety, which was very undadlike behavior.

"No, that's it."

"So how was the movie?" It had been a long time since I'd struggled to make conversation with my dad. Up to this point, we'd shared an easy camaraderie.

"We didn't go," Dad admitted. "Blythe said she had a headache, so I dropped her at her house and came home."

Interesting. "That's too bad."

"She's feeling better now," Dad informed me.

"That's good." I began petting Tucker, who had wandered over to say hi.

"I heard the movie didn't really get very good reviews anyway."

"Yeah, I'd heard that too." I felt like I was speaking to a stranger.

"There are a couple coming out next week that look like they might be good."

"Maybe you can reschedule your date."

"Yeah, maybe." This conversation, I decided, was completely ridiculous. I decided to retreat before I broke into tears. "I guess I should get going."

"Yeah, okay. And thanks again."

"Call me when you want me to bring the kids home."

"Okay. Will do."

I stood up and started toward the door. I turned to hug my dad, as I always did when I left. He embraced me with stiff arms that felt completely foreign to the loving ones I'd known all my life.

"Are you ever sorry you didn't have more kids?" I asked.

"What?" My dad looked shocked by the question, which I suppose was a normal response since my inquiry had come from out of the blue. "Why would you ask that?"

"No reason." I shrugged. "I guess I was just curious."

His face softened. "I would love to have had more children if they were all exactly like you. There are times the idea crossed my mind, but I'm not sorry it was just the two of us, if that's what you're getting at."

I hugged my dad again and he hugged me back. A real hug this time, not like the artificial ones we'd been sharing since Blythe arrived in our lives.

"I know this whole thing with Blythe is hard for you, but I want you to remember that you will always be my number-one girl."

"Thanks, Dad. I love you too."

As I loaded the dogs into the truck and started home, I fought the sinking feeling in the pit of my stomach that genuine encounters with my dad were going to diminish if he married Blythe. Somehow I had to figure out how the shewitch was connected to the murders and then prove it.

Levi and Ellie both texted me several times during the day to ask if I wanted to get together that evening to work on the murder case. I couldn't very well tell them that I'd been doing just that all day without hurting their feelings, and if I suddenly acted like the urgency I'd expressed the previous day had somehow evaporated, they'd find that suspicious as well. After discussing it with Mom and Zak—I can't tell you how much I love any sentence that includes the phrase *Mom and Zak*—we decided I'd invite Levi and Ellie to the boathouse that evening and we'd work on the case together. We decided to take Charlie and Lambda with us and leave Tucker and Kiva with Mom.

"Thanks for coming," I said, greeting Ellie as she arrived ahead of Levi. "Zak and I needed some time to discuss a few things, but I've been anxious to get back to the case of my serial- killer stepmom-to-be."

"Your dad and Blythe aren't actually engaged," Ellie pointed out.

"I know, but I have a feeling it's only a matter of time."

"So things are good? With you and Zak?"

"Yeah, things are good." I smiled.

Ellie hugged me. The one thing you can say about Ellie's hugs is that they're never artificial or less than 100 percent heartfelt. "I'm glad," she whispered in my ear. "If there were ever two people destined to be together, it's the two of you."

"How about you?" I asked Ellie as the hug ended and I took a step back. "Have you decided what to do with your brotherly love triangle?"

"I spoke with Rick today. I explained that Rob and I were just friends at this point, but that I really liked spending time with him and would like the opportunity to see where, if anywhere, our relationship might go. He told me that he was fine with that. He said that his comment the other night was impulsive, and he realized we'd already had our time as a couple. He's not looking for anything serious, so our relationship really had nowhere to go. He warned me that Rob *is* looking for a serious relationship, though, and he asked me if that was what I wanted."

"And do you?"

"Do you what?" Levi asked as he stomped the snow from his boots after letting himself in through the front door.

"I was just asking Ellie if she was interested in a serious relationship at this point in her life," I informed Levi.

"Of course she's not. Are you, El?"

"I might be open to something along those lines," Ellie countered. "With the right guy."

Levi frowned. "Are you talking about Rob? I thought you were just friends."

"We are," Ellie confirmed. "For now."

Levi got the strangest look on his face. A look that made me wonder if he was into Ellie more than he let on.

"How are things going with Barbie?" Ellie asked.

Levi took off his jacket and hung it on the coatrack by the door. "If I said horrific, I'm afraid that would be putting it mildly."

"She still mad?" I wondered.

"*Mad* is much too tame a word. I really thought she'd shrug the whole thing off and move on to the next guy, but instead she's turned into a raving lunatic."

"Oh no. What did she do?" I asked.

"I guess in all the flying dishes the other day, I neglected to get my key back. When I got home from the gym this morning, I was greeted with fabric squares on the floor of the living room."

"Fabric squares?"

"The fabulous B must have thought I needed a new wardrobe because she let herself in and cut almost all of the clothes I own into little squares. Luckily, she didn't think to check the laundry, so I have a few things left. It's going to cost a fortune to replace everything she destroyed."

"Ouch."

"Ouch is right. Not only did she destroy my clothes but she took a bat to my television. That girl is bad news."

"Did you call Salinger?" Ellie asked.

"No. For one thing, I don't actually have any proof she did it. For another, I just want to put this all behind me."

"It sounds like she could be dangerous," I pointed out.

"I changed the locks. If she comes back, I'll call the cops. Where's Zak?"

"He went to pick up Chinese food. He should be back in a few minutes."

"So have you made any progress on the case?" Levi asked.

"A bit." I filled them in on everything we'd learned to date, including the fact that Blythe had been married before.

"It does seem odd that she would tell you that she'd been a teacher if she hadn't," Levi said. "And I agree that if she'd been a teacher, she would most likely have been fingerprinted. Everyone who works in our school system has to not only be printed but also has to undergo an extensive background check."

"Maybe she worked for a private school," Ellie suggested.

"Perhaps," I admitted.

"You can just ask her where she taught," Ellie proposed.

"Trust me when I tell you that the least amount of time I have to spend with that woman, the better. Still, if I happen to get trapped in her company again, I guess I can ask her."

"I'm not sure I'm quite as convinced as you are that your dad's girlfriend is the demon you think she is, but it does seem like there are some inconsistencies where she's concerned," Ellie commented.

"She's staying with Dad this week," I informed my friends. "Dad asked me to watch his dogs while Blythe has her house fumigated."

"Who fumigates in the middle of winter?" Levi asked.

"I know! Right? That's exactly what I thought. I really get the feeling that she's just looking for an excuse to be at his house on a full-time basis."

"You think she plans to check in but never check out," Ellie guessed.

"It makes sense. She wants to live with my dad and he's hesitant. I wouldn't put it past her one bit to worm her way in."

"Yeah, but your dad loves Tucker and Kiva," Ellie pointed out. "I can't see him giving them up altogether."

"Yeah," I said. "I know you're right. Still, it doesn't mean Blythe won't try to get rid of them."

"You don't think she'd . . ."

I knew exactly where Ellie was headed. "I think she'd do whatever she needed to do to have things work out the way she seems determined for them to work out."

"The whole thing gives me the creeps," Ellie said with a shiver.

"Tell me about it. I'm not sure exactly how I'm going to accomplish it, but I promise she'll be gone from our lives by the end of the month."

Zak and I decided to return to his house after Levi and Ellie left. Now that I knew my mom was there, I didn't feel right about leaving her alone, and I certainly wasn't going to spend any more nights away from Zak, so we decided I'd just stay with him for the time being. We packed up the cats, and Zak, Charlie, Lambda and I made the short trip down the beach. After we got everyone settled in, we decided to take a nice long soak in the hot tub.

"This is so nice," I sighed as I laid back my head and looked up at the stars. The weather had held, so Zak had started a fire in the indoor/outdoor fireplace and retracted the roof of the pool room. There were billions of stars twinkling in the night sky like diamonds on a dark background.

"More champagne?" Zak asked before topping off my glass.

"I'd love some."

"I've been thinking about doing this ever since you mentioned it the other day." Zak set the now empty bottle aside and began kissing my neck.

"I have to admit I was pretty devastated when you suggested we go out instead." I groaned as he made his way just a bit lower.

"I know." Zak continued to kiss me. "Keeping my promise to your mom and lying to you was one of the hardest things I've ever had to do."

"Good." I grinned. "I wouldn't have wanted lying to me to be easy for you."

"Never." He found my lips.

"I've been thinking about the fact that I'm going to have a hard time," I said as Zak ran a finger along my jaw.

"A hard time?" Zak prompted.

"Lying to my dad," I managed to finish the sentence. "I think the best thing that can happen is if we facilitate a meeting between the two.

"The best thing that can happen?" Zak nibbled on my ear.

"Well, maybe not the *best*."

Chapter 8

Sunday, February 9

The next day was Sunday and I had nowhere I had to be. The shelter was closed, and Jeremy had agreed to go in to tend to the few animals we hadn't yet placed. Zak and I had shared an amazing night and I had spent most of my sleeping hours dreaming about picking up exactly where we left off. I rolled over and reached for the man of my fantasies only to find an empty bed.

"Zak?" I opened my eyes. The sky was blue and the sun was reflecting brightly off the freshly fallen snow outside the bedroom window.

I looked around, but the room was obviously empty. Even Charlie was gone. I quickly dressed, then hurried downstairs to find out what was so important that it had compelled Zak to leave me alone in his big bed.

I heard the sound of their laughter before I saw them. Apparently, Mom and Zak were in the kitchen, and based on the sound of dishes being moved, combined with the giggling coming from the room, I had to assume they were making breakfast while having a tickle fight.

"Morning, sweetheart," Mom called to me. "I hope we didn't wake you."

"No, I woke up on my own. What's going on?" I focused my attention on Zak.

"I woke up early, and Madison was awake as well, so we decided to make breakfast."

"Is it a funny breakfast?" I couldn't believe I was actually jealous of my own very pregnant mother, who was sitting on the window seat with Marlow and Spade.

"Zak was just telling me some stories about you as a teen," Mom filled me in. "They were really pretty funny. I can't believe how much I missed."

"Don't worry." I sat down on one of the bar stools lining the kitchen counter. "I'm still pretty hilarious, so I doubt you missed much. What are you making?" I asked Zak.

"Omelets?"

"Sounds good. Where are the dogs?"

"I let them out in the yard." Unlike my yard, which has no fence, Zak's estate was completely enclosed in the front of the house, although it was open in the back, where the lawn met the beach. "We can let them in after they work off some of their energy. Four dogs make for quite a commotion the first thing in the morning." Zak set a cup of coffee in front of me.

"I've already eaten, so I think I'll go up and get dressed," Mom informed me.

"Do you have plans for the day?" I asked Zak as I sipped my coffee and Mom waddled away.

"Some interesting information came up as a result of my background search for Blythe Spalding," Zak informed me. "I thought I'd follow up on it."

"Interesting how?"

"Blythe had been married at least once before getting hitched to Tim Ravenwood. I found a wedding license from 2007, when Blythe Bonham married Peter Spalding."

"Okay, so what happened to Peter?"

"He died."

Now I was really feeling bad for Blythe, and I didn't like the feeling one bit. "How did he die?"

"Allergic reaction to peanuts."

I frowned. "I know accidents happen, but aren't people who are allergic to peanuts usually really careful about what they eat?"

"Usually, but I guess you can never know for sure if something was cooked on the same grill or in the same pan."

"I realize it's possible to be widowed twice in four years, but doesn't it seem an odd coincidence to you?"

"Actually, yes," Zak agreed. "For the first time, I almost believe you might be onto something regarding your suspicion of Blythe."

"I told you." I felt a sense of victory as Zak slipped bread into the toaster.

"Told you what?" Mom walked back into the room with the dogs on her heels.

"We found out that Blythe has been married twice. Both husbands died, one from a heart attack and one from an allergic reaction to peanuts. Zak was just saying that he's beginning to believe I might have grounds for my distrust of Blythe."

"Do you think Hank could be in danger?" Mom paled.

"It's doubtful," Zak assured her. "Still, it wouldn't be a bad idea to keep checking."

Mom sat down on the bar stool next to me. She was so tiny and petite that her belly looked like she'd tucked a basketball up under her shirt. I hoped that I'd be as cute and compact as she was if and when I decided to have a baby. The idea of having children had always horrified me, but as I watched Zak making my breakfast, even taking the time to cut the crust off the toast as I preferred, I realized that never wanting a child might have evolved into maybe wanting a child. Someday, that is.

"Okay, so now what?" I asked as I attempted to redirect my thoughts.

"I can continue to backtrack," Zak suggested. "Try to find out where Blythe Bonham came from."

He slid a golden omelet onto a plate and placed it in front of me. I cut off a bite and sighed as a delightful yet unusual combination of tastes exploded in my mouth. "What did you put in this?' I took a second bite. "It's delicious."

"Secret recipe," Zak teased.

"You never should have made this for me. Now I'm going to insist that you cook for me *every* morning."

"I'd be happy to."

I smiled.

"You should try Zak's sticky buns," I told my mom. "He made them for Thanksgiving and they were to die for."

"I'll have to request some while I'm here."

"I'm not trying to be pushy," I finished the last bite of the omelet, "but have you given any thought to what you're going to do? In the long run, I mean."

"Not really." Mom sighed. "I guess I figured I'd talk to your dad and then take it from there."

"I can call him and invite him to come over."

"No. Not yet. Maybe after we figure out this whole thing with Blythe."

"As I was saying," Zak rejoined the conversation we'd been having before we got sidetracked, "maybe it would be a good idea if we kept on checking into Blythe's background."

"Now that Zoe is finished with her breakfast, why don't we move this to the living room?" Mom suggested. "I don't want to miss anything, but my back is killing me, so I thought I'd stretch out on one of the sofas."

"You have a problem with backaches?" I asked.

"Yeah. I'm afraid this pregnancy has been a lot harder than the first one. I'm not exactly a spring chicken anymore."

"Forty-two isn't old."

"It is to have a baby."

"Yeah, I suppose."

I sat on one of the sofas while Mom stretched out on another. Zak sat at the table where he'd set up one of his many laptops. Mom and I talked about her pregnancy and my new little sister while he typed away.

"The doctor thinks everything is going okay?"

"He does. I've had a few scares, but Zak has been really great about helping me through them. I texted him the other day because I was having strange cramping. He was home within fifteen minutes and had me to the doctor before I could change my clothes."

I realized that must have been the reason he'd left me so abruptly at lunch.

"When Zak told me the two of you were dating, I couldn't have been happier. He's a good man."

"Yeah," I agreed, "he is."

"I'm not sure what I would have done without him," Mom admitted. "I don't know if I could have done this on my own."

"I'm glad Zak has been there for you, but you also have me now," I reminded her.

Mom brushed a stray hair off my face. She smiled. "I do have you. I should have told you sooner."

"Yes," I scolded, "you should have. And you should tell Dad," I tried again. "He'll be hurt that you didn't."

"But what if he's mad?" Mom looked scared. "What if he never forgives me for messing up his life?"

I held Mom's hand in my own. "Trust me: he won't be mad and he won't think you messed up his life. In fact, if I know Dad the way I think I do, he'll be thrilled."

"You think so?"

"I really, really do."

"I have the computer searching for any information it can dig up on Blythe Bonham," Zak interrupted. "It might take a while. Blythe was a Bonham before every move a person made was recorded via the Internet highway. I could really use a break," Zak decided. "It's stopped snowing for now, but there's another storm on the way, so I think I'll head into town and get some more ice cream. It seems a certain individual," Zak looked at my mom, "who shall remain nameless, has already plowed through the four cartons I bought a few days ago."

"Chunky Monkey," Mom requested. "And peanut butter chip."

"I think we're out of yogurt as well," Zak said, starting to make a list.

"And cookies," Mom added.

I have to admit that watching my mom and Zak as they made the list with an easygoing casualness I had never had with my mother made me feel left out in a way I'm certain neither intended. I wasn't sure how all this would play out, but I was happy to have my mom in my life, even if it didn't turn out to be a forever thing.

"So how are you doing?" Zak asked as we drove toward town in his truck.

"Honestly? I'm not sure," I admitted. "Having my mother in town after not having seen her for such a long time is . . ." I searched for the right word, "confusing. I love my mom and I'm thrilled to have some time with her. It's just that the joy I feel over her being here is all mixed up with the fear that it will be twice as hard when she leaves and discomfort with lying to my dad. We both know that my mom's track record for sticking around is dismal. And now I won't have only her to miss if she leaves but my new baby sister as well. I guess the whole thing leaves me feeling unsettled."

"Your feelings are understandable." Zak held my hand across the bench seat. "As long as you've settled Charlie and the cats at my place, you might as well stay for a while. At least until we can convince your mom to talk to your dad. It will give the two of you a chance to catch up."

"I'd like that. Have the two of you talked much since she's been here?" I asked.

"Not really. At least not about anything important. We've shared stories about quaint little restaurants we both enjoy in Europe and places we've both visited. Stuff like that. She's bounced a few baby names off me, but I don't think any of them are names she intends to use."

"Like what?"

"Ambrosia, Mirabella, and Chanterelle, to name a few."

"They're all pretty but sort of long. I guess they could be shortened to nicknames like Amber, Belle, and Elle."

"What would you name her if given a choice?" Zak asked.

"I really don't know. I think that, ideally, a name should have meaning. Having said that, it still needs to be a cool name. Something not too ordinary, but not strange either."

"Like Zoe."

"Exactly."

"Does Zoe have special meaning?" Zak asked as we pulled into the parking lot of the grocery store.

"Not as far as I know, but my middle name is Harlow, which is sort of a mash-up of my Grandma Donovan's name, which was Harriett, and my pappy's name, which is Lowell."

"Zoe Harlow Donovan. It's nice. But I thought Pappy's name was Luke."

"Luke is his middle name. Lowell is a family name, which I guess has been around for generations. Pappy's gone by Luke since he was a kid. What's your middle name?" I wondered.

"Zion."

"You're kidding? Zak Zion Zimmerman? Your parents were really into Zs," I said as I climbed out of the truck.

"Actually, it's Zachary Zion Zimmerman, but yeah, it's a mouthful. Maybe a mash-up of your dad and mom's name would work for little sis," Zak suggested.

"My dad's first name is Lowell, like Pappy's and, like Pappy, he goes by his middle name, which is Harold. Well, he goes by Hank, which is normally short for Henry, but Pappy didn't like Harry as a nickname for Harold, so he started calling dad Hank when he was little and it stuck. My mom's name is Madison. I'm not sure what you could get from either Madison-Lowell or Madison-Harold. Although," I realized, "if you combine the *Har* from Harold and the *Per* from my mom's middle name, which is Perletta, you get *Harper*."

"Harper is nice."

"Yeah." I smiled. "It is. I think I'll suggest it to Mom."

The parking lot was deserted. It was already well into Sunday afternoon, and most folks were probably home with family. Zak and I held hands as we walked across the hard-packed snow to the front door of the market. Zak grabbed a red rolling cart as I paused once again at the chocolates on display.

"I guess 'tis the season for chocolate." Zak tossed a couple of boxes into the basket.

"I'm not sure we needed a cart for a few cartons of ice cream."

"I figure we could pick up some other supplies as long as we're here."

Grocery shopping with Zak was really romantic. We'd never actually shopped together before, and it was fun to discuss what brand of toothpaste to buy and what kind of cereal provided the most fiber. As we strolled up and down the aisles, I realized that I had probably learned more about Zak in the half hour we were in the store than I had in all the time I'd known him.

"I can't believe you're so opinionated about laundry detergent," I teased.

"A good detergent mixed with a quality presoak product can make all the difference in dealing with difficult stains."

I laughed.

"Take this presoak." Zak picked up a bottle. "This one claims to instantly melt away any stain within minutes, and based on the exorbitant price, most people would feel they were buying a quality product, but the truth is that this stuff works about as well as water. This stain lifter, on the other hand," he said, turning to a much less expensive bottle, "works every time."

"You spend a lot of time presoaking?"

"Just call me the laundry master."

I rolled my eyes, but it seemed Zak also had quite a few strong opinions on everything from toilet paper to produce.

"We should do this more often," I suggested as we made our way to the checkout. "It's fun to get a peek inside your complicated brain."

"We can make a weekly date of it."

I had to admit I'd never known anyone as diversified as Zak. He seemed to know a lot about pretty much everything. As I watched the hundreds of dollars' worth of groceries Zak bought glide by on the conveyer belt, I felt my phone vibrate in my pocket. I looked at the caller ID but didn't recognize the number.

"Hello," I said, prepared to hang up at the first sign of a telemarketer.

"Zoe," someone cried. "It's Kevin. He's been arrested."

"What?"

"Please come. No one else can help me."

"Kevin Michaels has been arrested," I said to Zak as soon as I hung up. "His wife is beside herself. I told Maureen we'd come by their house as soon as we could get there."

"Don't take this the wrong way, but why would she call you? Are the two of you close?"

"We aren't," I agreed. "I guess Kevin might have mentioned to her that I'd been asking around about Trent's murder."

"Yeah, I guess that makes sense. We'll drop this stuff off at my house and head over there."

"Maureen," I said, holding the hysterical woman in my arms less than an hour later. "I understand that you're upset, but you need to calm down and tell us what happened if you want us to help you."

Maureen pulled back and took several deep breaths. Zak handed her a tissue and a glass of water. "Okay," she hiccupped.

"Why don't we sit at the dining table?" I suggested.

"Sorry about the mess." Maureen began to straighten up the things on the table. "Things have been hectic and I haven't had a chance to get to the housework."

"No problem." I felt empathy for the poor woman, who hurriedly ran a cloth over the table and picked up several clumps of thick red mud from her carpet.

"Seems the vacuuming is never done with a contractor in the family." She blushed. "If Kevin isn't tracking in mud from a construction site, it's sawdust from the mill."

"I have three animals, so you don't have to apologize to me. Charlie seems to be a mud magnet. If there's one tiny puddle, he'll find it."

Maureen smiled.

After everyone had taken a seat, I said, "Now tell us exactly what happened."

"Sheriff Salinger came by a while ago. He said he had a warrant to arrest Kevin for Anthony Martucci's death. That's crazy. Kevin would never kill anyone."

"Did they say why they suspected him?" Zak asked.

"Something about the murder weapon belonging to Kevin. I was so upset, I didn't catch everything."

"I'm going to call a lawyer I know," Zak announced.

"We don't have a lot of money."

"Don't worry. Moses is a friend of mine. He'll be able to get the story a lot quicker than we can."

I made Maureen tea while Zak talked to the lawyer. Poor Maureen was beside herself. I tried to get her to sit and talk, but she wanted to pace, and pace she did; back and forth, endlessly, across the living room. Zak was probably only on the phone for two minutes, but with all the wailing and pacing, it seemed more like two hours. I could understand why

Maureen would be upset that her husband had been arrested, but the degree of her distress seemed melodramatic and somehow contrived.

"Is your friend going to help?" Maureen asked the minute Zak hung up the phone.

"Yeah. He's going to call Salinger to see what he can find out and call me back when he has news. In the meantime, let's go over everything you know. Any detail, no matter how small, could be relevant."

"What do you want to know?" Maureen twisted the tissue she was holding until it was shredded.

"I guess the obvious starting point is to establish an alibi," I began. "Anthony Martucci died Sunday evening. Do you know where Kevin was then?"

"He was here with me. All night," Maureen assured us.

"How would you describe Kevin's relationship with Trent?" I asked.

"Kevin liked Trent. They got along very well. In fact, Trent came by once a week or so for dinner. He particularly loved some of the things I made from recipes I learned from Mom. Kevin is a finicky eater, so I didn't make them often, but once I realized Trent and I shared similar tastes, I started having him to dinner more often."

"Did Trent ever mention his life before he moved to Ashton Falls?" I asked.

"Not really. I'm pretty sure he was instructed not to speak about it."

"Did Kevin tell you how he came to hire Trent?" Zak wanted to know.

"Yeah, he filled me in on the Fresh Start program. He figured I should know about it before he agreed to participate."

"Do you happen to know why Kevin was approached about the program in the first place?" I realized that might have been a good question for me to ask Kevin when I'd had the chance.

"No, he never said," Maureen answered. "Kevin said that the prison system was looking for a small, out-of-the-way town where Trent could disappear, and since they'd trained him in construction, I guess Kevin was a logical choice."

"And Kevin wasn't told what Trent had done to end up in prison?" I clarified.

"No, other than the fact that he was involved with a bad crowd."

Zak's cell rang as Maureen and I spoke. He excused himself to take the call, which he informed us was from Moses.

It occurred to me that it might be worth our while to have Zak check into the Fresh Start program. When Kevin had first mentioned it, it had seemed to make sense, but the more I thought about it, I had a harder time believing that anyone would take someone into their life without being aware of the *specific* reason they'd gone to prison in the first place.

"I think the best way to help Kevin is to figure out who *did* kill Anthony Martucci," I told Maureen. "Can you think of anything? Anything at all that might point us in a direction?"

"Not really. Kevin and I were both very upset when we found out about Trent. We might have felt the urge to hurt the man who killed him, but I can assure you that neither of us acted on it. It's natural to feel rage when someone you care about is needlessly slaughtered. It's possible that someone else in the community who Trent had helped out and gotten to know might have felt that same rage."

I thought about Willa, Tawny, Old Man Johnson, and Mary Grayson. None of them seemed like the type to kill a man. I had the feeling there was something important I was missing, but I couldn't quite put my finger on what it could be.

"So?" I asked as soon as Zak walked back into the room. Maureen still looked like she might pass out.

"Anthony Martucci was hit over the head with a pipe wrench. The sheriff thinks whoever killed him was in the room when Martucci arrived. It appears the killer hit Martucci with the wrench and then threw it into the Dumpster behind the motel, where it was found. The weapon had both Anthony's blood and Kevin's fingerprints on it."

"Oh God." Maureen went white.

"According to what Moses could find out, Kevin claims he lent the wrench to Trent over a week ago and hasn't seen it since," Zak added. "Kevin believes someone is setting him up. The problem is, Salinger talked to a couple of his workers, who said that Martucci came by the Mendoza worksite to talk to Kevin a few days before the murder. And several people saw Kevin arguing with him the day before he died."

"What now?" I asked.

"There's nothing we can do today. I'm going to suggest we pick this up tomorrow," Zak said.

"Is there someone we can call for you?" I asked Maureen.

"My neighbor. Her number is by the phone."

After the neighbor arrived, Zak and I got back in his truck and headed toward his house. "Did it seem like Maureen knew something she wasn't telling us?"

He nodded. "I got the feeling that her answers were guarded. She called *you,* so I'm not sure why she'd lie to us, but there was definitely more going on than she would admit to."

"I want to believe that Kevin didn't kill Martucci, but it's starting to bother me that there are a few too many holes in the story. For one thing, if, as Kevin suggested to Moses, someone went to the Zoo, found Trent's body, realized that Martucci must have killed him, and then decided to kill him but frame Kevin for the murder, they would have had to have been in possession of a whole lot of information." I began to count off facts on my fingers. "First of all, they would have had to have known that Trent was going to be at the Zoo. Second, they would have had to have known that Kevin's wrench was in Trent's possession *and* have had access to his tools. And thirdly, they would have had to have known that Martucci was looking for Trent, that there was reason to suspect him of killing Trent, *and* know where Martucci was staying. There really is only one logical suspect."

"Kevin," Zak agreed. "So what now? Do we continue to try to prove Kevin's innocence?"

"I don't know," I admitted. "Maybe we should go by to talk to him tomorrow. Maybe he knows something he hasn't mentioned yet."

Chapter 9

Monday, February 10

By the time we'd gotten home the previous day, Zak and I were physically and emotionally exhausted. I fed the cats while Zak let the dogs out, and then we both fell into his big bed and a restless slumber. When we got up the next morning, we filled Mom in as best we could and headed into town.

Jeremy had called asking for help, so Zak went to speak to Moses to see, what, if anything, we could do to help Kevin and I headed to the Zoo, where my assistant was knee deep in pets and people. Apparently, despite our slow start, now that people knew we were open, it was raining cats and dogs. Even with Jeremy's colorful description of the chaos at the Zoo, I wasn't entirely prepared for the line outside the door that greeted me.

"All these people have animals they want to turn in?" I asked.

"Most want to adopt, a few are just lookie loos, but a few actually have animals to place."

"So where did all the animals come from?" I wondered as I walked down the hall and viewed the full cages.

"Once the other shelters in the area heard we were accepting overflow, they started sending them faster than I can process them. I have people who want to adopt many of the new arrivals, but I need to check them in and have Scott give them shots and exams before we can release them."

"Didn't the shelters they came from have their shots updated?"

"Most did, but like I said, I need to go through all the paperwork and see what's what."

"Okay, one of us will work the desk and the other will check in the new animals. Which do you want?"

"Honestly, as much as I normally hate paperwork, I had a rough night last night and could use the peace and quiet of doing the intakes."

"Too much partying?"

"Too much baby-mama drama. I'll tell you about it later."

"Mulligan's after closing? My treat."

"Sounds perfect."

Jeremy headed into the office, where we kept our files, computers, and other business equipment, and I headed toward the front counter. "Can I have everyone's attention?" I yelled. "While I am thrilled that so many of you turned out for what appears to be our second grand opening, I'm afraid we're in a bit of a bind as far as our paperwork is concerned. I'd like to have two lines. If you're here to adopt, please step to the left; if you're here to drop off, please step forward, and if you're here to see the place, please come back tomorrow and I promise to not only give you the grand tour but to provide refreshments as well."

After my speech, more than half of the people standing around left. I called Pappy and asked if he could bring over doughnuts and coffee for those who had chosen to wait. He did, and everyone seemed to enjoy the "adoption party," as each potential adoptive parent discussed what they hoped to find in the new animals that had arrived. Only four people were dropping animals off. Normally, four in one day would be unheard of, but we'd been closed since the first of November, and people were waiting to leave their animals with us rather than take them to the kill shelter in the valley.

"And who do we have here?" I asked Phyllis King, a member of the book club at the senior center.

"This is Tazzy," she said, handing me a long-hair black cat. "She's really sweet, but she doesn't get along with my Annabelle. When my neighbor moved and couldn't take him, I promised to give it a try, but it simply isn't working. I've asked around, but Tazzy has some bad habits and is really a one-pet cat, so I haven't had much luck. His shots are current and he's been neutered."

Tazzy really was a beautiful cat, but he hissed at me when I accepted him from Phyllis, and the long scratch where he dug his claws into my arm quickly started to turn red. "I'm sure we can find someone who will be just right for him," I assured Phyllis.

The next intake was a man who had gotten a Saint Bernard as a Christmas gift for his daughter and claimed he had no idea how big he would get. It's amazing how many big dogs are brought in because the owner saw a cute puppy and didn't bother to research the specifics of the breed. I refrained from giving my do-the-research-before-you-adopt speech and instead handed the man a pamphlet on the different breeds: their size, temperament, and special needs.

The next dog was a Doberman who hadn't been properly socialized and was aggressive, followed by a poodle puppy Mom had bought but Dad wanted nothing to do with. While I hate to see an animal who doesn't work out with a family, I'd much rather they come to us so that we can properly place them than have them remain in a high-stress, abusive, or otherwise undesirable situation.

Once I'd completed the intakes, I began to interview potential adoptive families. There's a misconception that all it takes to adopt an animal is to show up with the proper fee and take home a pet that night. Many shelters do it that way, but I've always been of the mind that if I make a careful placement the first time, I won't see the animal back in a few weeks. Some potential dog and cat families are well versed in the tasks of pet ownership and know exactly what they want, while others . . . Let's just say I tend to be concerned when someone comes in and asks for a white dog or a big dog, without knowing anything about the breed they're adopting.

"How's it going?" Jeremy asked after I had completed the intakes and started on the adoptions.

"Really good. We have some excellent candidates."

"Any going home today?"

"I told Silvia she could take that sheltie that was brought in with the animals from Bryton Lake last week and Hazel that she could take the black kitten. Silvia's an experienced dog owner who has had a sheltie before, and Hazel has been waiting for a kitten to be eligible for adoption for quite some time. Other than that, I told almost everyone I'd call them tomorrow or the next day. I'd like to get a chance to meet the animals and look over the applications."

"Sounds like a plan," Jeremy answered. "Now that you've finished with the interviews, you can finish the paperwork and I'll clean the cages and exercise the dogs."

"That's why we make such a good team. You're always willing to do the dirty work."

After we closed up for the evening, we headed over to Mulligan's. I was tempted to call Zak to ask him to join us, but Jeremy seemed to want to talk and I wanted to be there for him.

"So what's up on the baby front?" I asked as I paid for the beer and an order of artichoke dip in a bread bowl. Jeremy had just turned twenty-one a few weeks earlier, and I was still getting used to the fact that he could join me for an after-work cocktail.

"Gina is just so uncomfortable and so unhappy, and she blames me for it all. I've tried to be there for her, but last night she went completely off the deep end. She was so hysterical that I didn't feel like I could leave her alone. It's really not like her to be so irrational."

"Pregnancy hormones can wreak havoc with some women," I cautioned. "Add that to the fact that she never wanted the baby and I'm sure she's finding herself regretting her decision. You, my friend, make an obvious target for her anger."

"Yeah, I guess. I just hate to think about how Gina's anger is affecting Morgan."

"Maybe Gina needs a break. Does she have any friends who might be willing to go on a trip with her?"

"She's in her seventh month. I don't think she should be traveling. Although to be honest, I think that's part of the problem. Gina has always traveled a lot. She's used to having a busy life. She doesn't have a lot of friends, so she ends up sitting home all day by herself. By the time I check in with her every evening, she's totally worked up and wants to kill me."

"Let me think about it. Maybe I can come up with something. In the meantime, be patient with her. I've never been pregnant, but I understand that it can be very uncomfortable."

I realized as I spoke to Jeremy that hooking up Gina with my mom might be a good idea. My mom was more than twenty years older than Gina, so not an obvious friend, but both had traveled extensively and enjoyed being pampered and partaking of the finer things in life. My mom was at Zak's all day, most times alone. I'm sure she could use the company and if nothing else, Gina would enjoy the facilities the extravagant estate afforded. Not only was there an indoor pool and workout room but there was a fully equipped spa that my grandmother had used when she was in residence. She'd had a staff to administer the spa treatments, but I was willing to bet there was someone who could be hired to come in on a temporary basis.

Of course, I'd need to discuss the idea with Mom first, so I refilled Jeremy's beer and turned the conversation to baby buggies and bassinettes. By the time we—mostly Jeremy—had finished off the pitcher of beer, Zak had wandered in looking for me. We decided it best to drive Jeremy home rather than risk a DUI, so Zak took him while I ran over to the boathouse to pick up some more clothes before meeting back at his place.

When I arrived at Zak's, he was pulling into the drive with takeout bags from one of my favorite Mexican places. Mom hadn't eaten yet, so the three of us sat down at the kitchen table and dug into the delicious food. I told Zak about my day and the plethora of animals that had shown up, and he shared that Moses has spent most of the day looking for legal precedents while he'd been busy helping a client through a software nightmare.

"It seems," Zak continued, "that if we believe Kevin is innocent and want to help him, our best chance of getting him off the hook is to figure out what really happened."

I cut off a bite of cheesy enchilada and popped it into my mouth as I thought. "We know that Martucci most likely came to town looking for Trent, or maybe I should say Joey. We know Trent was part of a relocation program. Do we know what he was arrested for?"

"Double homicide," Zak informed me.

"Homicide? Sweet, giving Trent killed someone?"

"Two someones," Zak confirmed. "Joey Marino was involved in the gangland murder of two members of a rival Mafia family when he was just sixteen He was tried as an adult due to the severity of the crime and sentenced to a good, long time in prison. According to his parole officer, once he was isolated from the influence of his family, he began to see the error of his way and eventually agreed to provide sensitive information to law enforcement in exchange for an early release."

"I'm guessing the family he ratted out found him." I felt bad for Trent. He'd had a rough start in life, but based on the little I'd found out about him, he seemed to genuinely want to live a helpful and honorable life.

"It looks like Anthony Martucci was some type of enforcer for a Mafia family based in New York."

"Mary told me she'd overheard Trent talking to someone named Bruno, who apparently had spoken to someone named Giovanni."

"Giovanni Lombardi is the name of the head of the family Joey Marino was connected with," Zak confirmed.

"That fits. Mary said it sounded like Trent feared this man, but also held him in reverence."

"Okay, so Martucci catches up with Trent and kills him for betraying the family. So who killed Martucci?" Mom asked.

"That's the million-dollar question," I said.

Chapter 10

Tuesday, February 11

I knew we were going to be slammed again at the Zoo on Tuesday, and Zak had a conference call with one of his contacts in Europe early in the day, so he arranged to meet with Kevin at the jail after we closed for the day. I arrived at the Zoo early enough to process many of the applications I'd received the previous day and was able to evaluate six of the requested animals to the point at which I felt comfortable calling the prospective doggy parents and telling them that they'd been cleared to pick up their new family members.

"Does it seem odd to you that we've had so many applicants?" Jeremy asked. "I realize we've been closed for a few months, but we placed a lot of animals before we closed, and we had the adoption clinic in December. I'm amazed we got one new application, little alone twelve."

"Yeah, I'm as surprised as anyone," I had to admit. "I suppose people might have gotten caught up in the opening-day frenzy. I know I bought a bunch of clothes I didn't need and wouldn't otherwise have bought when the new mall in Bryton Lake opened."

"I guess, but these are animals and not clothes that can be easily returned."

"That's why I'm taking my time processing the apps. Gives folks time to really think about it, and change their minds if they realize they aren't ready for a new family member."

"That Doberman we took in yesterday is a real grouch," Jeremy informed me. "I think we might want to blacklist him from the adoption pool until we can work with him a bit. I'm afraid he might bite someone."

"Yeah, let's do that," I agreed. "I'll try to spend some extra time with him. If we can get him some training and teach him to relax, I think he'll be fine."

"And the cat who scratched you?" Jeremy asked.

"We need to find him a placement with an experienced pet owner who doesn't currently have any other pets."

"That's going to be hard to do."

"Yeah, but we have to try. Any word on the cubs from the Anderson fire?"

"Being delivered as soon as Salinger releases our bear cage."

"They haven't had any luck getting them to hibernate?"

"Their weight is too low, so they don't want to risk it."

"Okay. I'll call Salinger to see what I can do," I promised. "Go ahead and arrange for transport. The sooner we get the little guys settled, the better. If Salinger won't release the bear cage, we can always set something up in one of the other pens."

The rest of the day flew by. As promised, I gave those who showed up both a tour and a snack, but luckily, we didn't have any additional drop-offs or adoption applications to deal with, and as unbelievable as it may seem, Salinger actually cleared us to house the cubs in the bear cage. I guess he figured he had his killer, so the investigation, in his mind, was all wrapped up.

After I got off, I ran home to change. Zak picked me up as planned and we headed over to have a conversation with Kevin. I was actually surprised that Salinger had agreed to let us talk to Kevin, but perhaps Moses had worked some of his magic in our absence. Zak and I were shown to a room and told to sit on one side of the table, while Kevin was ushered in and instructed to sit on the other.

"Do you have any news?" Kevin asked.

"Nothing good, unfortunately," Zak said. "If someone intentionally set you up, they did a good job of it. I know this must be stressful for you, but we really need to go through everything again."

"Yeah, okay, whatever you need. I can't thank you enough for trying to help me."

"Okay, let's go back over exactly how you got involved with Trent," Zak started.

"I received a phone call from a woman who said she had an inmate to place as part of the Fresh Start program and asked if I would be interested in participating. She assured me that the individual in question had been trained in all aspects of construction, and that the state was going to cover his salary for the first six months. If he worked out, I agreed to hire him as an employee and take over his salary. It seemed like a good idea, so I agreed to meet him. We hit it off right away."

"Did they tell you anything about his past or the charges against him?"

"Not specifically."

"So you agreed to the arrangement, and then what?" Zak continued.

"He was brought to Ashton Falls by a parole officer. Initially, he rented a room from Willa Walton, and then eventually got his own apartment. He was a quiet sort who did an excellent job, and I'm pretty sure he never missed a single day of work."

"Were you aware that he did jobs on the side?" I asked.

"Yeah, he told me about it. He wanted to help out folks who couldn't afford to pay me for the work they needed done. I figured I wasn't going to get the work anyway, so what the heck? He always worked on his own time, so it didn't cost me anything."

"You said you lent him your pipe wrench," Zak said.

"Yeah. He had some of his own tools, but he needed to borrow mine from time to time. He always returned them when he was done. I'm pretty sure he mentioned helping Mary Grayson with some plumbing."

"Is it reasonable to assume he had the wrench with him when he went to the Zoo to work on the electrical panel?"

"Yeah. He wouldn't have needed it for that job, but he kept his tools in a box in his pickup. I suppose it's possible he could have left it unlocked when he got the tools he *did* need."

"If we're going to continue to operate under the assumption that someone intentionally set you up, then whoever took the wrench would have to have known it belonged to you."

"My initials are chiseled into the handle. I do that with all my tools. Stuff gets left lying around on job sites, and I don't want a misunderstanding as to who owns which tool."

"Still," I chimed in, "if the killer got the wrench out of Trent's toolbox, he or she must have been looking for it specifically. Otherwise why not just grab a hammer, and there was a large ratchet next to the panel Trent was working on in the Zoo too. Who else, other than you, knew Trent had your pipe wrench?"

Kevin sat quietly while he thought about it. "Trent asked me if he could borrow it on Friday, after we'd finished for the day. He told me that he'd need it over the weekend for a big job, so he might need to keep it for a few extra days. I told him I was planning on going on a ski trip with some buddies, so I wouldn't need it. We were just finishing up a remodel and I was feeling pretty good because the homeowner had promised me a big bonus if I could get it done in record time, so I figured I might just take a day off to myself."

"Did anyone see you lend the wrench to Trent?"

"No. It was the end of the day and the rest of the crew had gone home. It's possible someone saw the wrench and noticed the initials on it during the time Trent had it."

"True," Zak acknowledged. "Let's move on to the first visit you had from Anthony Martucci at the Mendoza job site."

"He was looking for someone named Joey Marino. He said he had reason to believe he was working for me. I denied knowing anyone by that name, but I suspected it might be Trent. I asked Trent about it. He didn't confirm or deny that he was this

Joey, but he did mumble something about Bruno and his big mouth."

"And then you ran into Martucci at the market."

"Yeah. He asked about Joey again, and I assured him that I'd never heard of him. He told me where he was staying and asked me to contact him if I thought of anything." Kevin paled. "I guess that's pretty bad. It proves I knew where to find him."

"Yeah," Zak admitted, "it's not going to help your case."

"Did you mention this to anyone?" I asked.

"No."

"I'm going to keep working on this," Zak promised. "But if you think of anyone who knew that Trent had borrowed your wrench *and* that Trent would be at the Zoo that night *and* where Martucci was staying, it will go a long way toward giving us a new direction."

"There's no one," Kevin realized. "Based on this information, I have to be the killer, but I swear to you that I'm not. Besides, if I *had* killed Anthony Martucci, why would I mention to Zoe where he was staying? And why would I simply throw a wrench with my initials on it into a Dumpster? I would think that the total absurdity of the situation should prove that I'm the victim here."

Kevin had a point. Maybe too good a point.

Zak and I discussed the case as we drove home. The roads were icy, and I knew I should let Zak focus all of his attention on his driving, but I couldn't seem to keep myself from verbalizing my thoughts as I tried to work the whole thing out. "The only explanation I can come up with regarding how this whole thing could have come together other than Kevin being the killer is that someone followed Trent to the Zoo and watched him get his tools from his toolbox. They would have had to be watching as first Willa came by, and then Tawny. After they left, the killer had to have seen Martucci go in. He or she heard the gunshot, realized what happened, grabbed the wrench out of the toolbox, and followed Martucci back to his motel."

"Not only is that theory far-fetched but unrealistic," Zak pointed out. "First of all, you told me that Pack Rat saw everything up to the time Martucci went inside. If there was someone else watching Trent, Pack Rat would have seen them. Besides, if someone heard the shot and got out of their car to get the wrench, Martucci would have been gone by the time his killer got back to their car. He or she couldn't have followed him back to his motel."

"True," I admitted. "It really does seem that Kevin could be the only one to pull this off."

"Or Pack Rat," Zak suggested. "He admitted to being there the whole time. What if he didn't leave after Martucci went inside? What if he waited, heard the shot, and followed Martucci?"

"Pack Rat doesn't have a car."

"Then I guess we're back to square one." Zak sighed.

Chapter 11

Thursday, February 13

Wednesday flew by in a blur. Things were crazy busy at the Zoo, and Zak was crazy busy trying to juggle his work commitments and helping Moses get Kevin freed. We got up early and came home late. The pace was definitely cutting into our *us* time, but at least we had the nights. The short but glorious nights. I felt bad that Mom was home alone all day. I spoke to her about Gina, but although she was not adverse to the idea of company, she insisted that until she told Dad her news, she didn't want anyone else to know she was in town.

Luckily, today seemed to be settling into a slower pace. I worked most of the morning helping Jeremy with the cleanup and finalizing the remaining adoptions, and then decided to cut out early to spend some time with Mom. Jeremy promised to call if things got busy, so Charlie and I picked up some takeout and headed back to Zak's.

"I can't believe Dad's dogs are still here," I commented as we chowed down on burgers. "He loves them. It's really not like him to leave them for so long."

"I guess this must mean Blythe is still at his house." Mom sighed.

"If you want to get rid of her, we should tell Dad about the baby," I suggested.

"What if he's mad?"

"He won't be."

"But what if he is? What if he wants nothing to do with either of us?"

"When you got pregnant before, he was the one who stayed," I reminded her.

"Yeah, but he was a lot younger then. We both were. And he didn't have a girlfriend."

"Look, you've already decided to tell him at some point. Why not do it now? If he's mad, he's mad, but I can guarantee he won't be. I'm betting he'll be thrilled."

Mom looked doubtful.

"Can you think of any reason to wait?" I asked.

"No," Mom admitted. "I guess waiting won't lessen the shock."

"Then tell him now. Today. I'll call him and invite him over."

Mom hesitated.

"If he gets engaged to Blythe or, worse yet, moves in with her, it's going to be twice as hard to tell him."

"Okay."

"Okay?" I smiled.

"Yeah. I might as well get it over with."

"I'll call Zak. He'll want to be here. And then I'll invite Dad to dinner."

"What if he brings Blythe?"

"I'll tell him I have something private to discuss and want him to come alone."

I can't tell you how excited I was about the fact that Mom and Dad and my baby sister and I were going to be a real family. I had dreamed my entire life of all of us living together, and now, for the first time,

I felt like my most secret wish was going to come true. Not that I was going to move in with them, but Mom and Dad and Harper—Mom loved the name—would live together and I would visit my whole and happy family often.

I called Dad and he agreed to come to dinner alone. I went into town and picked up the most tender fillets I could find. I bought veggies and potatoes and champagne for the majority of us, as well as sparkling cider for Mom. I made my special artichoke dip for an appetizer and mini cherry cheesecakes for dessert. I used Grandma Montgomery's dishes, which Zak had bought with the house, to set the table. I added fresh flowers and the best crystal to the table. Everything was perfect, like a fantasy come to life. I couldn't remember the last time I was this happy and excited about anything.

I even changed into a dress, and Mom put on a red velvet jumper that accentuated both her belly and the rest of her perfect, petite frame. My heart pounded with excitement as Dad pulled into the drive. I opened the door and waited on the porch for him to get out.

"Wow, you look nice. I didn't know this was formal."

"It's not." I hugged my dad, who was dressed in a sweater and soft cords. "I'm just in a really good mood and wanted to dress up a bit."

Dad hugged me back. "I can't wait to hear your news."

"You're going to be so surprised."

"Not really." He smiled. "I always knew you and Zak would end up together."

"What?" I pulled back. "This isn't about me and Zak."

"Then why the fancy getup?"

I took Dad by the arm and walked him through the door. I knew Mom was waiting with Zak just inside. "This is way better than an engagement announcement," I assured him. I opened the door. "Mom's here."

I'm not sure what I expected. Whooping and hollering. Jumping for joy. A passionate reunion between two people who had always loved each other but had wasted a lifetime apart. What I didn't expected was stunned silence.

"Hank," my mom nervously uttered.

My dad just stared at her.

"Surprise," she said weakly and started to cry as Dad remained motionless.

"We're having a baby," I joined in.

"I can see that," Dad finally responded. He looked at Mom with shock on his face. "It's mine?"

"It is." Mom looked like she might pass out, and Dad looked like he might turn and run away. Maybe I'd overestimated how wonderful he'd think the news was.

"You should have told me."

I didn't like the hardness in Dad's expression.

"I know." Mom began to sob.

Dad turned to look at me. "How long have you known?"

"A few days. I wanted to tell you, but . . ."

Dad looked at all of us like we were aliens, turned, and walked away.

"I don't know why you expected your dad to be thrilled with the news right off the bat," Zak commented as he grilled the steaks I no longer felt like eating. Mom had gone upstairs after Dad left and hadn't come down since.

"I just figured he'd be as thrilled as I was to have Mom back."

"Your parents have a long and complicated history. A history, if you remember, that has brought mostly pain to your dad. He's finally moved on with his life after twenty-five years of waiting for her to return his love, and she shows up seven months pregnant."

"You could have mentioned this before now," I accused.

"I did. When you called and told me your plans, I said I thought it was a bad idea to spring things on your dad like this, and that it made more sense to ease him into the reality of another child."

"Yeah, but you could have stopped me from making a mess."

"I've never been able to stop you from making a mess," Zak reminded me. "All I can do is clean up after you."

I stuck out my tongue at the man I loved. He wasn't wrong, but it was rude to point it out. "I've never seen my dad so mad."

"I don't think he was mad. I think he was in shock. Your mom has had months to think about things and get used to the idea. She ran away when she found out. I think you should cut your dad some slack. Give him a chance to get used to the idea."

"Yeah," I sighed, "you're right."

"Give him a day or two and then call him."

"Poor Mom. She looked like she was going to pass out."

"She's been stressing over telling your dad for months. I'm sure she hoped for a different reaction, but I'm betting she's happy to have everything out in the open. We'll make her a plate and you can take it up to her. If she doesn't want to talk, though, don't force it. Maybe she needs a little time as well."

Chapter 12

Friday, February 14

To say that I didn't sleep well would indicate that I slept at all, and the truth of the matter was I didn't sleep that night. I got up, as was my routine, and went into work, but after one look at me, Jeremy sent me home. I'd tried to talk to my mom last night, but she'd feigned fatigue and told me that she was turning in early. She hadn't come down by the time I left for work, and Zak had reminded me to give her the space she needed.

When I got back to Zak's, he was gone. Mom was up and informed me that he had a meeting with Moses to discuss a possible defense for Kevin if we weren't able to discover the real killer. All I really wanted to do was go upstairs and sleep for a year, but the table I'd so carefully set the previous evening was still covered with dishes; unused, but still best put away. I began gathering the linen napkins I'd so carefully ironed the previous day. I dropped one, and when I bent down to retrieve it, I noticed several sheets of paper on the floor under the table Zak had been using as a desk.

I picked them up and was preparing to place them on top of the computer when I noticed Blythe's name. I realized that I held the background check Zak had left running when we'd gone to the store the day we'd found out about Kevin's arrest. I'd forgotten all about it, and I bet Zak had as well. The computer Zak used for work was located in his office upstairs, and he had a laptop that he kept locked in his truck. I doubted he'd even come back to the computer we'd used on that Sunday afternoon. I looked at the report and tried to decide what I was looking at.

As we'd discovered before, Blythe had married Tim Ravenwood in 2010. Tim had died of a heart attack in 2011. Prior to that, she had been married to a man by the name of Peter Spalding. They'd married in 2007 and Peter died as a result of an allergic reaction to peanuts in 2008. This much we'd uncovered before the search. Zak had been trying to find out about Blythe Bonham prior to her marriage to Spalding. I scanned the sheet. As odd as it may seem, it appeared Blythe Fox had married William Bonham in November 2004, and he'd died in 2005.

"What are you doing?" Mom asked as she joined me from upstairs.

"Looking over the report Zak ran on Sunday."

"I'd forgotten all about that."

"Me too. Look at this. Blythe was married to someone named William Bonham before Peter Spalding."

"Three marriages? Seems like a lot, but I suppose not unheard of in this day and age."

"Make that four," I continued to read. "Blythe Brenner married Owen Fox in November 2001."

"I guess Blythe had commitment issues, with that many divorces under her belt."

I got a terrified sinking feeling in my stomach as the facts before me began to sink in. "All four men died," I informed her.

"Wow, what are the odds?"

"Astronomical," I supposed. "Owen Fox fell off the roof, William Bonham was killed in a single-car accident, Peter Spalding died from an allergic reaction to peanuts, and Tim Ravenwood died from a heart attack. Oh God."

"What?"

I looked at Mom. "Blythe married all the men in November and all of them died three months later." I took a deep breath and tried to calm my nerves. "They all died on Valentine's Day."

"Hank!"

"I have to warn him." I ran for my truck keys.

"But your dad isn't married to Blythe."

"I know, but all the deaths are exactly three years apart, and the last death was in 2011. Call Zak and tell him what's going on. Tell him to meet me at Dad's."

"Maybe you should just call the sheriff," Mom suggested.

"Dad could be dead before I convinced Salinger we have a real situation. I'm going." I hugged my mom.

"Be careful," Mom said, hugging me back. "Maybe you should take the dogs."

"No. Blythe knows I know she doesn't like the dogs. I'm hoping she won't suspect I'm onto her until after I manage to neutralize her."

I'm sure I broke every traffic law on the books as I sped toward my dad's. I prayed the entire time that I wouldn't be too late. I slowed down as I got to Dad's street so as not to alert her. I got out of the truck and casually made my way up to the front door. I knocked, but no one answered. After what seemed like hours but was probably less than a minute, Blythe came to the door.

"Zoe, what are you doing here?"

"I just came to talk to my dad."

Blythe paused as she tried to make up her mind about something. "He's in the den. You can go on back."

I walked down the hall with Blythe behind me. The door was closed, so I opened it. I gasped as I saw my dad lying on the floor, blood dripping from his forehead.

"Don't worry, he's alive. For now," Blythe said from her position behind me.

I turned, and for the first time I noticed the gun in her hand.

"What did you do?" I accused.

"I tried to get him to go down into the basement. He resisted, fell, and hit his head. If you don't want me to shoot both of you, you'll wake him up and get him to go with you."

"So you can kill us like you killed the others?" I grabbed some tissue and held it to my dad's head.

"Found out about that, did you? You certainly are a nosy little thing."

"Why Dad? You aren't even married."

"Yes, that is unfortunate. It really is upsetting to me that the pattern has been altered. I was engaged to a man by the name of Vernon Claven. We were to be married in November. I married them all in November, on the eighth. The idiot had to go and get himself killed in a climbing accident last September. It totally messed up my timeline."

"Why move to Ashton Falls?"

"I ran into a friend of the family who told me about the place."

"And why my dad?"

"I just happened to run into him. He seemed vulnerable. It seems your mom had recently left, and he was open to moving things along at a brisk pace. I might have gotten him to marry me if it hadn't been for you. I didn't plan to kill you as well, but I find I'm looking forward to it quite a lot. Now wake up your dad and get downstairs."

I didn't know why Blythe didn't kill us right then, but given the fact that she was a raving psychopath, I assumed she had some sort of twisted ritual she needed to perform first. I gently nudged Dad, and thankfully, he opened his eyes.

"Zoe, what are you doing here?"

"Just stopped by to chat," I said, trying for a light tone. "It seems your demon girlfriend wants us to go down into the basement."

Dad looked confused. I was pretty sure he was suffering from shock and blood loss. He allowed me to help him up and I escorted him down the stairs. I could hear Stepwitch lock the door behind us. I reached for my phone but realized it must have fallen out of my pocket as I helped Dad.

"What's going on?" Dad asked as he faded in and out of consciousness.

"Blythe locked us in the basement."

"Why?"

I shrugged. "I guess she's in a playful mood today." I figured it wouldn't do me any good to tell Dad that his girlfriend planned to kill us. Dad looked confused before he closed his eyes and passed out. I doubted he'd even remember the conversation.

I looked around the room. There was a small window at the very top of the wall to which my dad had added bars years ago. The room was below the surface of the ground, and soundproof as well. When I was in high school, I was a member of a garage band, and Dad had soundproofed the basement so we'd have a place to practice without disturbing the neighbors. I tried the lights, which didn't work. Psychowitch must have flipped the breaker. I figured we had two hours of light left and then we'd be locked in a totally dark room.

I sat down on top of an old trunk and tried to keep myself from panicking. My dad remained unconscious, and it occurred to me that you were supposed to keep people with head injuries awake, but if the devil woman upstairs was just going to kill us anyway, why put him through the agony? On the other hand, if we somehow managed to escape, I would have wished I'd kept him awake.

"Dad." I gently shook his shoulder. "Wake up, Dad." I brushed his blood-soaked hair from his head. "Please, I need you. I don't know what I'd do without you."

Dad stirred but didn't open his eyes.

"Please, Dad, I love you."

"Zoe?"

I helped Dad sit up. "You have a head injury; you need to stay awake."

"Blythe?"

"Locked us in the basement. She's planning to kill us."

"Kill us?"

"She's killed at least four other men. All on Valentines' Day. All three years apart. I was coming to rescue you, but I guess that didn't work out as well as I planned."

Dad looked confused, but luckily he didn't panic. He had started to shiver, so I began sorting through trunks, looking for blankets or old clothes to wrap him in. I'd forgotten all this stuff was down here. I found a trunk with blankets, propped my dad up against a wall, and made him as comfortable as possible.

"Your mom gave me this blanket." Dad smiled weakly. "It was shortly after we met. Before we found out about you. She told me it was to keep me warm when she couldn't be there. I slept with this blanket every night for the longest time. Even after she left. It made me feel close to her. "

I bit my lip to keep from crying. "I'm sorry about last night. I handled it poorly."

Dad patted the ground next to him. I sat down and rested my head on his shoulder.

"I'm the one who's sorry. I don't know why I reacted the way I did. I was in shock, I guess. Never in a million years did I expect your mom to be there, and I certainly had no idea about the pregnancy. There was just that one time."

"Apparently, just one time is all it takes," I teased.

"A baby," Dad whispered.

"A girl. Harper. My idea," I informed him. "I combined the *Har* from Harold and the *Per* from Perletta. I thought it would be nice for her to have something from each of her parents."

Tears began to stream down Dad's face.

"We can change it if you don't like it."

"I love it." He squeezed my hand.

"Don't worry; we'll get out of here," I assured him. "Mom called Zak. The guy is a genius. He'll figure something out. He always does."

"You love him."

"I do."

"Any wedding bells in the future?"

"I don't know. Maybe. But not now. The only thing I want to do right now is get out of here so I can be alive to meet my baby sister."

I looked around the basement. I hadn't been down here in ages. When I was a child, I played in the basement using the old furniture and boxes of mementos as props for a fantasyland in which only I existed. I had a lot of friends, but there has always been a part of me that likes to spend time alone with no one for company except my imagination.

"Remember when I was ten and we had that big fight about whether or not I could go to that party Jillian Prescott was having?" I knew it was important to keep Dad talking so he didn't drift off again.

"Jillian was thirteen. You had no business going to a middle-school party."

"I know that now, but at the time all I knew was that I had been invited to the biggest party of the year and there was no way I was going to miss it. I was so mad when you said I couldn't go. I came down here and hid."

Dad smiled. "I looked everywhere for you. I thought you had run away. I even called the sheriff."

"I know. I was so scared. It was like my tantrum got away from me. At first I was happy that you were worried about me. I figured it would teach you to think twice before saying no to me. And then I saw the sheriff pull up out front and I got so scared. I thought he was going to arrest me."

"I'm pretty sure your little stunt drained a good five years off my life."

I hugged Dad's arm. "When I finally worked up the courage to come upstairs, you were so happy to see me that you weren't even mad. At first," I qualified. "I do seem to remember a month-long grounding once your relief wore off."

"There's nothing worse as a parent than to have a missing child. For all I knew, you were injured or kidnapped."

Dad began to shiver again, so I got up to look for additional blankets while we continued to chat.

"And then there was that time you helped me build that princess castle in my bedroom. You built a frame, and Grandma made a drape to put over it. I slept on the floor in that castle for at least a year."

"That was after you'd visited your mom. She lived in that big house with the pool and horse stables, and she had a staff that took care of the cooking and cleaning, and you were convinced she must really be some sort of a princess if she could have such fabulous things. When your grandfather's aide brought you back to me, you insisted that if your mom was a princess, then you must be too, and insisted on having a castle. I couldn't give you a real one, although believe me, I wished at the time that I could. I built the one in your room and you seemed happy. I think you were five, or maybe six."

"Was it hard for you to let me visit Mom?" I asked as I continued to go through boxes of long-forgotten treasures.

"Yes and no. I wanted you to have a relationship with your mother, but I missed you when you were gone, and I always felt bad that I couldn't give you the same things when you came back with tales of swimming in her pool or learning to ride a horse."

"Yeah, but what you gave me was so much more." I held up a silver candlestick. As long as I was going through boxes, I figured I might as well search for something to use as a weapon if I was given the chance to use it. "I visited Mom, but you were the one who never left. I think Mom really wants to be a better mother this time around."

"When is she due?" Dad asked as I considered whether silver candlesticks or crystal goblets would work better as a means of self-defense.

"April."

"And everything is going well?"

"She says this pregnancy has been harder on her than when she was pregnant with me, but she seems to be doing okay."

"I sure hope we get out of here." Dad sounded scared. "I'd hate to miss watching Harper grow up. Being a father to you is the most important thing I've done in my life. Now that you don't need me anymore, I find I'm really looking forward to having another opinionated, impulsive, and intuitive daughter to raise."

I found a blanket and wrapped it around Dad's shoulders. He continued to shiver, and I began to suspect that the shivering had more to do with shock than the cold.

"You know how much I like being right," I teased, "but I really am sorry I was right this time. I know you cared for Blythe."

"I was lost when your mom left last fall. Blythe came along and filled a void. I never really loved her, but I've been alone my entire life and it felt right to have someone to come home to. These past few years since you've moved out have been lonely. Although"—Dad groaned as he adjusted his position, and I could see he was in pain—"I do suppose that being alone is preferable to shacking up with a killer."

I snuggled up to Dad as close as I could. I willed my body to share its warmth with the person who meant more to me than anyone else on the planet.

"I guess we've all had dates from hell," I teased. "Remember when I was totally into Drake Bitterman?"

"That hippie wannabe who wore tank tops, bell bottoms, and sandals, even in the winter? He talked about free love, finding yourself, and living without the constraints of modern mores. I was so worried you'd marry him and move to a commune or something. I'm not sure I ever saw the guy when he wasn't high. Whatever happened to him?"

"He made millions of dollars selling medical marijuana. The last time I saw him, he was wearing a suit and heading for a medical conference."

Dad laughed. "I guess you never can tell about people."

"Yeah, I guess not."

Dad stiffened. "Did you hear that?"

"Yeah." I listened. "It sounds like voices." The voices were coming through the heating vent, but they weren't loud enough to make out. "I bet it's Zak."

"I hope he won't end up down here with us."

"He's much smarter than I am. I doubt he'll come waltzing in unarmed."

The voices quieted and I heard the door close.

"Whoever it was left," Dad said.

"Yeah, it might have been a door-to-door salesman for all we know."

Dad let out a deep breath. I could tell he was beginning to lose hope.

"Don't worry. The good guys always win," I promised.

"I love you." Dad looked directly into my eyes.

"I love you too."

"Whatever happens, I want you to know that having you in my life has made all the difference."

I was pretty sure I was going to cry, but then we heard a rustling coming from upstairs. Dad and I held hands as footsteps neared the basement door. We held our breath as it opened. Blythe stood at the top of the stairs with the gun she'd had earlier.

"As much as it disturbs me to do so, I guess we're going to need to hurry things along. I hate to end things early, but I really can't abide any more interruptions."

"Your real name is Adriana." I suppose that fact was irrelevant now, but my instinct told me to stall by keeping her talking.

"I had a feeling you weren't going to be convinced that Anthony simply made a mistake. I really hoped you'd drop it after Joey was killed and you got distracted with the murder case."

"You killed Trent?"

"No, Anthony took care of that for me." Blythe, or I guess I should say Adriana, chuckled.

"But you knew Trent, or I guess I should say Joey."

"I did," Blythe admitted. "Joey and I are from the same neighborhood in New York."

"You belonged to the same Mob family that Joey did," I realized.

"I married into the family. Giovanni Lombardi was my father-in-law, a position, I might add, that he was less than thrilled about. I made the mistake of falling in love with his oldest son, Russo. When Giovanni found out, he tried to break us up, but Russo told his father that if anything happened to me, he'd leave the family. Eventually, Giovanni gave in and blessed our union. Russo had to swear that he'd put the family first in all situations."

Blythe paused. I could tell she'd really loved Russo. Her face softened and the demon looked almost human for the first time since I'd met her. "Things were fine at first. I knew Russo was involved in illegal activities and that quite a few deaths in the area could be attributed directly to him, but I loved him and he loved me. He'd come home to me every night and I'd forget about the details of his day job. The problem started when my brother joined a rival family. Giovanni ordered Russo to kill him. Russo refused. Giovanni reminded him that he'd sworn to put the family first, and that he wouldn't let his marriage to me interfere with his duties to them. When he still refused, Giovanni killed my husband right in front of me, on Valentine's Day. I guess he felt he needed to send a message, but I loved Russo so very much."

Oh God. "And Joey?" I asked.

"Joey was just a kid at the time of Russo's death, but he recognized me when we ran into each other a while back. We both wanted to hide from Giovanni, so when he told me about this place where it was easy to get lost, I moved here. I guess I admired the fact that he stood up to the family by ratting them out. I've hated those people for years. I only wish I could have had the courage to do something about it."

"So you killed innocent men instead?" Dad chimed in.

"I didn't start off intending to kill anyone. It happened with the first one by accident, and then it got easier. It was Valentine's Day, the anniversary of Russo's death. I'd married Owen, a man I didn't love but found companionship with, the previous November. He made my life a bit more tolerable, but as Valentine's Day approached, I began to resent the fact that he was alive and Russo was dead. I was so terribly despondent by the time February 14 finally rolled around. Instead of enjoying what I had with Owen, I mourned the love I *should* have had. There was a storm, and Owen went onto the roof to clear an exhaust pipe. I followed him and pushed him. I didn't intend to do it when I started up to the roof. I guess I just gave into an impulse, but I found the experience to be completely cathartic. I felt better than I had since Russo's death."

"Why every three years?" I wondered.

"Russo and I were married for three years before Giovanni took him from me."

Blythe got a look on her face that could only be described as mournful. She'd really loved Russo. I couldn't imagine how traumatic it must have been to watch her father-in-law kill his own son in front of her because he refused to kill her brother. I felt momentarily sad for her until I remembered that she intended to kill us.

"You killed Anthony Martucci," I asserted.

"That was the plan, but someone beat me to it. Now that's enough chitchat. Both of you, stand up and face the wall."

"It seems like shooting us lacks the imagination you put into the other deaths," I spouted off. "No one is ever going to buy the fact that this was an accident."

"I had something much more imaginative planned for your dad until you showed up and ruined everything. Now get up and face the wall."

I held Dad's hand as we stood up. "If you're going to shoot me, you'll have to look me in the eye," I said as I refused to turn around.

"Very well." Blythe pointed the gun at us. I held my breath as she screamed and fell down the stairs. The gun flew out of her hand and I ran to get it. Zak stood at the top of the stairs, a look of relief on his face. He rushed down the stairs and hugged me.

"Are you okay?" Zak ran his arms up and down my body to make certain I was in one piece.

"I'm okay, but Dad . . ." I turned around. My dad had passed out again.

"The ambulance is on the way," Zak assured me.

"You heard?"

"I heard most of what Blythe said," Zak confirmed. "I even recorded it with my phone. I guess this pretty much wraps things up."

"With a single missing piece," I reminded Zak. "Who killed Anthony Martucci?"

Zak looked directly into my eyes. "I think we both know the answer to that."

"Yeah." I sighed. "I guess we do."

"I've called Salinger," Zak said. "He's on his way as well. If you want to go with your dad, I can talk to him and let him know that he can speak to you there if he needs to."

"Yeah, okay, thanks."

Zak kissed me. "I'm sorry. I know you really believed he was innocent."

"Actually," I admitted, "it's not so much that I believed it, it was more that I *wanted to* believe it."

"I know. Me too."

Shortly after Zak arrived, the ambulance showed up and took my dad to the hospital. I went with him, while Zak went back to his house to pick up my mom, who'd insisted on going to the hospital when she heard what had happened to Dad. Once Dad had been checked out and we were assured that he was going to be okay, Zak and I headed over to the sheriff's office to file a report, as Salinger had requested.

Dad's head injury was actually fairly minor, but they wanted to keep him for a day or two for observation. Mom wanted to stay with Dad for a while, so Dr. Westlake volunteered to bring her home when he got off at nine.

"Thank you for coming," Salinger greeted us. "How's your dad?"

"He'll be okay. They're going to keep him for a couple of days, but he should be as good as new once his head injury heals." I looked directly at Salinger. "I guess you were right about Kevin." It pretty much killed me to admit that I'd been wrong and Salinger had been right, but fair is fair.

"Actually, I'm not so sure that I am. I've just received the official ME's report. The coroner has placed Anthony Martucci's time of death at between eight and nine-thirty p.m. on Sunday evening. According to two different sources, Kevin didn't return home from his ski trip until ten p.m."

"So he couldn't have done it," I said. "Then who?"

"We've brought Maureen Michaels in for questioning. She's denying that she's involved in any way, but the clues we've been able to assemble seem to point to her. The problem is that we don't have any real proof, so unless we can come up with something substantial, we'll have to cut her loose," Salinger admitted. "I was hoping you might have something that could help us nail down the case."

"She lied," I realized. "Why would she lie?"

"Care to elaborate?" Salinger asked.

"When Zak and I asked her about an alibi for Kevin, she said they were together all night. If Kevin was out of town until ten, then she lied. I should have realized it. I knew Kevin had gone skiing. It was the reason Trent was at the Zoo on Sunday night in the first place. God, I'm so mentally challenged."

Salinger laughed. "There were many instances when I would have agreed with your assessment of your mental capabilities, but in this case, I think you should give yourself a break. You didn't yet know the timeline for Martucci's murder, so you probably didn't give a second thought to Maureen's alibi for Kevin, and you've had a lot on your mind with the opening of the Zoo and what not."

I couldn't believe Salinger was actually being nice to me. Maybe he wasn't the lowlife scumbag I'd always thought he was.

"I did some checking, and it turns out that although there's a prisoner Fresh Start program of sorts, Joey Marino was never a part of it," Salinger continued. "Kevin admitted that Joey is actually Maureen's younger brother."

"Of course. Mom's recipes."

"Recipes?" Salinger asked.

"When we spoke to Maureen, she mentioned that she and Trent both enjoyed Mom's recipes. She said 'Mom's' recipes, rather than '*my* mom's' recipes. Maureen must be Reenie."

"Reenie?" Salinger asked.

"A couple of the people I talked to mentioned that Trent spoke of someone named Reenie from time to time. Trent, or I guess I should say Joey, was quite a bit younger than Maureen, so chances are that Reenie was Joey's nickname for his big sister. So why the ruse about the Fresh Start program?"

"According to Kevin, after Joey was released from prison, Maureen talked Kevin into giving him a job. They decided they didn't want to advertise the fact that they were related, so they made up the story about a Fresh Start program. When Anthony Martucci showed up looking for Joey, Kevin suspected they were in trouble. Kevin admitted he spoke to Martucci at the job site on the Friday before Trent's death, and then again the following day at the market. He had already planned to go skiing with friends on Sunday, so after Joey assured him that he'd leave town as soon as he finished a couple of jobs he'd already committed to *and* kept a low profile until then, Kevin went ahead and followed through with his plans."

"So why do you suspect Maureen?" I asked.

"She's the only one other than Kevin who knew that Trent was Joey and that Martucci was in town to find Joey, and that Joey had Kevin's wrench, and where Martucci was staying. If Kevin was out of town, Maureen has to be the killer. When I suggested this to Kevin, he didn't disagree. He said Maureen and Joey grew up in a highly dysfunctional family and Maureen more or less raised Joey. The two of them were very close, and Kevin admitted he wouldn't be at all surprised to discover that Maureen had taken revenge for her brother's murder. The problem is that all we have is a theory. We need some sort of physical evidence to link Maureen to the crime. We've swept the area for fingerprints, clothing fibers, anything we can dig up, but have come up empty. If Maureen did it, she was careful. I know you spoke to her and hoped you had some ideas."

"If Maureen did kill Martucci, it looks like she intentionally set up Kevin to take the fall. Why would she do that?" Zak asked.

"Kevin said there's been tension between the two of them ever since Joey came to Ashton Falls. Kevin was never a big fan of getting involved with his wife's brother. He was afraid that if Giovanni found out where Joey was hiding, it could put them in danger as well. When Martucci showed up, Kevin informed Maureen that he had asked Joey to move on, and she was livid that he would desert her only family. Maureen wanted Kevin to talk to me about having Martucci arrested, but Kevin realized that even if he *could* have gotten Martucci out of the way,

Giovanni would simply send someone else. Kevin thinks Maureen set him up as some sort of revenge for not trying harder to protect Joey. It seems far-fetched to me, but Kevin indicated that his wife is emotionally disturbed and might very well do such a thing."

I thought back to my conversation with Maureen. At first it didn't make sense that she'd call me for help if she was the actual killer, but the more I thought about it, I realized the distraught-wife act was actually a brilliant decoy. I thought about the entire conversation, moving through the events in my mind, trying to come up with anything that might help Salinger bring home his case. Maureen had been acting odd that day. The more I thought about it, the more certain I was that Salinger was actually on to something.

"If Maureen killed Martucci, she must have known that Joey was dead," I speculated.

"Possibly. Kevin has two theories. One is that Maureen went to the motel to kill Martucci as a way of protecting Joey. She might not have even known her brother was already dead when she did the deed. The other theory is that she went to the Zoo to talk to Joey, most likely to talk him out of leaving, or perhaps to talk him into taking her with him. She found Joey dead, realized that Martucci had killed him, and then went to the motel and killed Martucci with Kevin's wrench."

"If Kevin had come to you, could you have stopped Martucci?" I asked.

"Probably not. I couldn't have arrested Martucci based on nothing more than Kevin's opinion of his intent. Unfortunately, the law requires that I have proof that a crime has actually been committed before I can arrest someone. Which I guess brings us back to Maureen."

"The mud," I blurted.

"Mud?" Salinger asked.

"When we went to see Maureen, I noticed there was mud tracked on the floor. She made a comment about contractors and their muddy shoes, and how hard it was to keep the house clean. I didn't think anything about it at the time, but I just remembered getting mud on my shoes when I went to talk to Martucci at his motel. The same red mud that's actually not all that common in this area. I'm sure she's vacuumed, but maybe she hasn't cleaned her shoes."

Salinger thought about it. "Martucci was killed on Sunday, February 2. You spoke to Maureen a week later on the ninth. Do you think the mud could have been left on the floor for an entire week?"

"The place was a mess," I confirmed. "If I had to guess, there was at least two weeks' worth of grime on the floor and dust on the furniture."

"It'll be tough to arrest her for the mud alone, but maybe we can find a way to use it as leverage when we talk to her. You're correct in the fact that the red dirt found near the old mine where the motel was built is unique to that area."

"I'm happy I could help."

It was late by the time we returned home. It had been a long day at the end of a long week, and the only thing I wanted to do was sleep until I had to go to work on Monday, but I *did* have a killer dress for the Sweetheart Dance and I was certain Zak would look all 007 in his tux. I decided to take a long bath in Zak's huge tub to ease the tension in my body before washing and styling my hair. Luckily, I'd thought to bring my dress to Zak's, so all I'd need to do was muster enough energy so slip into it after applying a light dusting of makeup.

As I leaned back into the deep tub, I closed my eyes and thought about the surreal nature of the afternoon. Thankfully, Zak had had the presence of mind to pretend to leave my dad's house, only to slip back in after Blythe had started to go to the basement and pushed her down the steep stairs before she could shoot us. Blythe had been arrested for trying to kill us. She wasn't talking, but Zak had enough of what she'd said in the basement recorded that she had little chance of avoiding a good long stay in prison.

As I shampooed the long, curly hair Blythe hated so much, I thought about my mom and dad. They still had a lot to work out, but it appeared that they'd decided to try to slowly rebuild a relationship of some type, whether it be as friends or otherwise, while they prepared for the baby's birth. This might be wishful thinking, but if things did work out the way I hoped they would, baby sister Harper would grow up in the same home as both her mother *and* her father.

After drying my hair, I twisted it into a sloppy updo and applied just enough makeup to accentuate my features. I slipped into the floor-length red dress that hugged my frame and accentuated the few curves I actually had. I put on a pair of uncomfortable high heels and looked at myself in the full-length mirror. The dress was sleeveless and as thin as tissue paper, so I was certain I would freeze before I got to the dance. I was weighing the pros and cons of changing into something more practical when Zak walked into the bedroom.

"Wow." He simply stared.

"You like?" I asked nervously.

Zak started to respond but seemed uncertain what to say. "You look beautiful," he finally managed.

He walked across the room and tucked a stray lock of hair into the loose hairpins I'd used to try to get my mane under control. I shivered as his hand brushed my cheek.

"Maybe we should just stay in," he suggested.

"No way," I argued. "It took me two hours to transform myself into Cinderella and we're going to the ball."

Zak kissed my neck. I sighed.

"It *would* be a shame to waste the effort," he whispered as his kisses ventured lower.

"Hmm." I was becoming less and less interested in the conversation *and* less and less interested in the ball as Zak's kisses continued.

"Levi and Ellie are expecting us," I whispered.

"Then I guess we should go." Zak claimed my lips with his.

"Yeah." I groaned as Zak began massaging my bare back with his thumbs. "I suppose we should make an appearance."

"I guess we should."

"Or," I found myself weakening, "I could call them. I'm sure they'd understand."

"We could do that," Zak agreed. "Although," he said, "I think I hear the limo I ordered out front."

"Limo?"

Zak took a half step back and a deep breath. "I figured, only the best for Ashton Fall's most successful amateur sleuth. We can't have you showing up in a truck."

"You got me a limo? But I was totally wrong about Blythe being Martucci's killer."

A serious look came across Zak's face. "But you were right about Blythe being a killer. I'm sorry I didn't believe you when you insisted she was up to no good. My lack of faith could have gotten you killed. I need to start remembering that your instincts are usually right."

"Do you find that annoying?" I looked directly in the eyes of the man I was certain I couldn't live without. "A lot of men don't take kindly to a woman who insists on steering the boat."

"Oh, I like it when you steer the boat." Zak pulled me into his arms and kissed my neck. "I find"—he lowered his mouth just a bit—"your desire to steer the boat"—he found my mouth with his lips—"to be"—he whispered—"quite sexy."

I wrapped my arms around Zak's neck and showed him just how sexy I could be.

By the time we got to the dance, it was more than half over. Zak had ended up paying the limo driver a bunch of money to wait for us, but it had been worth it. I'd given up on the idea of redoing my hair and decided to wear it down in its usual wild style. When we arrived, Ellie and Rob were swaying as one on the dance floor, while Levi looked on with an irritated expression on his face.

"You here alone?" I asked. Zak had gone to get us some champagne.

"Wow. You look wow. What did you do with Zoe?"

"It's amazing the natural glow almost being killed can provide," I said with a laugh.

"You were almost killed?"

I filled him in on the highlights of the day while I waited for Zak to return from the bar. The last thing I wanted to think about was the monster who had almost gotten away with murder, but Levi had really helped me out and deserved to hear the end of the story. I looked around the community center as couples in love danced in each other's arms. The decorations were perfect and the music outstanding, but I found myself longing to be back home in Zak's big bed, or perhaps sharing the spa under the stars. I scanned the crowd, looking for the tall man with the broad shoulders and form-fitting tuxedo.

"Have you heard anything I said?" Levi asked.

"Hmm? Oh, sorry. I guess I'm just tired. What was that about Barbie?"

"She packed her stuff and left."

"Left? Where did she go?"

"I have no idea. I went by her place to once again try to get my key and a few things I left there, but her apartment was empty. Then I stopped by the yoga studio and they said she quit without giving notice."

"Well, at least you don't have to worry about any more attacks on your personal property."

"Yeah." Levi sighed. "I guess I'm glad she's gone, but it sucks being alone."

"Oh, please. You've only been alone like two minutes."

"I know. It's just that . . ." Levi looked out across the dance floor. "I really thought Ellie would change her mind and come to the dance with me."

I looked at my best friend wrapped in Rob's arms and then back at Levi. "You're jealous."

"What?" Levi spat. "I'm not jealous. It just would be nice to have someone to dance with."

"No," I insisted, "you're jealous. When you could have had Ellie you didn't want her, but now that Rob has her, you realize you don't like someone else playing with your favorite toy."

"That's ridiculous."

"I just calls 'em like I sees 'em."

"I'm not jealous of Ellie and Rob. I'm just not thrilled about being at the dance alone."

"Carly Wilder is here alone," I pointed out.

"Yeah, but Carly's not . . ." Levi paused. He looked at Ellie and then at me. "Maybe I *will* ask Carly to dance. You'll be okay alone?"

"Yeah. I see Zak coming this way."

Levi kissed me on the cheek. "You really do look spectacular. Zak is a lucky man."

"No, I'm the lucky one," I realized as the most perfect man in the room walked toward me with all eyes fixed on *him* while his eyes were glued solidly on *me*.

Recipes from Cupid's Curse

Artichoke Dip
Rosie's Clam Chowder
Ellie's Shredded Beef
Twice Baked Potato Casserole
Mini Cherry Cheesecake
Buttercream Chocolates

Artichoke Dip

2 cans (approx. 15 oz. each) artichoke hearts, drained and diced
1 can (approx. 7 oz.) Ortega or other diced green chili
1 cup mayonnaise
2 ½ cups grated parmesan cheese

Mix everything in a square baking dish and bake at 425 degrees for 35–40 minutes until bubbly and slightly browned on top.

Serve hot with French bread or tortilla chips.

Rosie's Clam Chowder

1 pound bacon
1 cup chopped leeks
1 cup chopped yellow onion
1 carrot, peeled and diced
Salt and pepper
1 tbs. chopped fresh thyme
½ cup flour
1 pound potatoes, peeled and diced
4 cups clam juice
2 cups heavy cream
2 pounds little neck clams, chopped
Parsley for garnish

In heavy pot, fry bacon until crispy. Stir in leeks, onion, and carrots. Sauté for about 2 minutes. Season with salt and pepper. Add thyme. Stir in flour and cook for 2 minutes. Add the potatoes. Stir in clam juice and bring to boil. Reduce to a simmer. Simmer until potatoes are tender and then add the cream. Bring to simmer and add clams.

Garnish with parsley and serve in bread bowls.

Ellie's Shredded Beef

Trim all fat off boneless rib roast (size depends on amount of meat desired). Season with salt, pepper, and garlic powder. Place in slow cooker. Cover meat with store-bought salsa (Ellie likes to use hot, but mild works as well).

Cook on high until meat begins to pull apart. Continue to shred meat as it cooks. When it is completely done (cooking time depends on size of meat and heat of slow cooker, but about 8 hours), spoon meat from sauce with slotted spoon.

Use as taco or burrito meat, or on top of creamy mashed potatoes.

Twice Baked Potato Casserole

5 medium to large russet potatoes, baked
10 pieces of bacon cooked crispy and crumbled
2 cups shredded cheddar cheese
1 cup grated Parmesan cheese
1 pint sour cream
½ cup green onion, chopped
Salt
Pepper

Either dice whole cooked potatoes or scoop out inner potato and discard skin. Combine with remaining ingredients. Transfer to greased baking dish. Bake at 350 degrees for 50 minutes until bubbly and lightly browned.

Mini Cherry Cheesecakes

Preheat oven to 350 degrees
Line cupcake pan with 12 liners

Crust:
1½ cups graham cracker crumbs (or crushed cookie crumbs)
6 tbs. butter or margarine, melted
6 tbs. sugar

Mix together and fill bottom of 12 cupcakes.

Filling:
2 (8 oz.) packages of cream cheese, softened
¾ cup white granulated sugar
2 eggs
2 tbs. vanilla

Mix together until smooth and free of lumps. Divide between 12 cupcakes. Bake at 350 for 15 minutes or until set.

Let mini cheesecakes cool completely, then top with cherry pie (or other fruit) filling.

Buttercream Chocolates

3 oz. cream cheese, softened
½ cup butter, softened
1½ tsp. vanilla
4 cups powdered sugar
2 cups chocolate chips
2 tbs. shortening

Beat together cream cheese and butter until smooth.
Mix in vanilla (other flavorings can be used for
variety). Gradually add powdered sugar until well
blended. Chill for an hour until firm. Shape into balls
and place on a waxed-paper-lined tray.

Refrigerate for at least 2 hours (overnight is better).

Melt chocolate chips and shortening in microwave or
double boiler, stirring frequently.

Using a toothpick, dip each buttercream center in
chocolate and place on waxed-paper-covered tray to
set. Refrigerate to hurry the process along, if desired.

Books by Kathi Daley

Buy them on Amazon today.

Paradise Lake Series:
Pumpkins in Paradise
Snowmen in Paradise
Bikinis in Paradise
Christmas in Paradise
Puppies in Paradise – *February 2015*

Zoe Donovan Mysteries:
Halloween Hijinks
The Trouble With Turkeys
Christmas Crazy
Cupid's Curse
Big Bunny Bump-off
Beach Blanket Barbie
Maui Madness
Derby Divas
Haunted Hamlet
Turkeys, Tuxes, and Tabbies
Christmas Cozy – *November 2014*
Alaskan Alliance – *December 2014*

Road to Christmas Romance:
Road to Christmas Past

Kathi Daley lives with her husband, kids, grandkids, and Bernese mountain dogs in beautiful Lake Tahoe. When she isn't writing, she likes to read (preferably at the beach or by the fire), cook (preferably something with chocolate or cheese), and garden (planting and planning, not weeding). She also enjoys spending time on the water when she's not hiking, biking, or snowshoeing the miles of desolate trails surrounding her home.

Kathi uses the mountain setting in which she lives, along with the animals (wild and domestic) that share her home, as inspiration for her cozy mysteries.

Visit Kathi:
Facebook at Kathi Daley Books
Twitter at Kathi Daley@kathidaley
Webpage www.kathidaley.com

Made in the USA
Middletown, DE
12 November 2014